NOTHI
CAN HURT
YOU NOW

'This is not your average neo-noir'
THE TIMES

'A high-octane, daring thriller'
STYLIST

'An original and welcome new voice'
FINANCIAL TIMES

'Gritty, raw and utterly fascinating... A fast-paced and gripping thriller'
SAMANTHA M. BAILEY

'Feisty, original and brilliantly crafted...
packed with memorable characters... [a] firestorm of a novel'
ROSE CARLYLE

'Real, flawed, complex women... [*Nothing Can Hurt You Now*] felt
totally different from most thrillers – in a good way'
TINA BAKER

'Sharp, subversive and surprising – everything I want from a thriller'
ELIZABETH LITTLE

SIMONE CAMPOS lives in Rio de Janeiro where she was born in 1983. Her literary debut, *No Shopping*, was released when she was 17, and since then she has published one short-story collection and four novels. She is also the translator of several English-language books into Brazilian Portuguese, including Paula Hawkins' *The Girl on the Train* and Margaret Atwood's *The Testaments*. This is her first thriller.

RAHUL BERY translates from Spanish and Portuguese and is based in Cardiff. He has translated novels by David Trueba and Afonso Cruz, and his shorter translations have appeared in *The White Review*, the *TLS*, *Granta*, *Words Without Borders*, *Freeman's* and *Partisan Hotel*. He was the British Library's translator in residence from 2018 to 2019.

NOTHING CAN HURT YOU NOW

SIMONE CAMPOS

TRANSLATED FROM THE PORTUGUESE BY RAHUL BERY

PUSHKIN VERTIGO

Pushkin Vertigo
An imprint of Pushkin Press
Somerset House, Strand
London WC2R 1LA

Copyright © 2019 Simone Campos
English translation © 2023 Rahul Bery
Published by special arrangement with Villas-Boas & Moss Literary Agency
& Consultancy and its duly appointed Co-Agent 2 Seas Literary Agency

Nothing Can Hurt You Now was first published as
Nada Vai Acontecer com Você in Brazil by Companhia das Letras in 2021

First published by Pushkin Press in 2023
This edition published 2024

Obra publicada com o apoio do Ministério das Relações Exteriores do Brasil
em conjunto com a Fundação Biblioteca Nacional – Ministério do Turismo
Work published with the support of the Ministry of Foreign Affairs of Brazil in
conjunction with the National Library Foundation – Ministry of Tourism

MINISTÉRIO DAS
RELAÇÕES EXTERIORES   BIBLIOTECA NACIONAL

1 3 5 7 9 8 6 4 2

ISBN 13: 978-1-78227-819-1

Designed and typeset by Tetragon, London
Printed and bound in the United Kingdom by Clays Ltd, Elcograf S.p.À.

www.pushkinpress.com

NOTHING CAN HURT YOU NOW

PROLOGUE

The billboard on the newspaper stand advertising the best Wi-Fi in Brazil seemed to bear no relation to the woman illustrating it, with her beaming smile and milky-white skin. She was smiling at the horizon, wearing a dainty white blouse, and looked like she was about to start talking. Lucinda imagined the snap being generated almost by chance during a change of pose at the shoot, as the model moved from a three-quarter profile to almost full-frontal. The photographer must have pointed over to where she should be looking – into eternity; she had obeyed and voila, the perfect photo, to be chosen from a multitude of others in which a thousand other girls in a thousand other nearly perfect poses would be passed over after test shoots of them standing next to the advertisement text.

Lucinda's attention was drawn to the corner of the image – *outside* it. At the edge of the stand, half-hidden by a strategically placed lamp post, a very pale young girl with brown hair and glasses was vigorously rubbing her face. Lucinda quickly realised that the girl was not alone and that she was rubbing her face in protest at the kiss her tall, slim, brown-skinned boyfriend had just planted on her nose. Her *nose*! The nerve! But her protests seemed to be in vain: the boy was determined to kiss unorthodox parts

of her face in public and was now laying into her cheek –
licking it! – before immediately returning to the nose.

What... am I looking at? thought Lucinda, accelerating
as soon as the lights changed. She couldn't get delayed
here; she had to get to that isolated point in the middle
of the highway as fast as possible. Perhaps in doing so she
would find her sister.

Viviana was not the woman in the advert. The woman
in the advert was white and a redhead; her sister, like
her, was mestizo: straight black hair, Indigenous features,
coppery-golden skin. She got her bronzed tone from sun-
bathing at her building's pool or country club; she didn't
like beaches. Lucinda spent all day in the office or at the
studio, feeding off artificial light.

Her sister was in advertisements, but not the kind that
appear on billboards, or on TV, or any other high-end
media. She had seen her sister on the back of a bus and
in a local newspaper; she frequently adorned web portals
and occasionally also dentists' brochures ('Your smile is
your calling card!').

Anyone who asked Viviana 'What do you do?' would be
unable to tell from the casual way in which she replied
'Model' that there was even the slightest hint of frustration with the fact that her face was considered perfectly
fine for illustrating materials on the sex lives of modern
couples, healthy food and the latest fashion trends, but
not for selling nationwide broadband, like the redhead
from the billboard. And it never, ever got her a speaking
part in a commercial, let alone a spot on the catwalk.

It hadn't always been that way.

8

• • •

Every afternoon Viviana (12) and Lucinda (16) would study French together at the language academy. The English they learnt at school was good enough, they didn't need any extra practice. The school they went to, private and highly esteemed, was obsessed with the word 'solidarity' and was always organising events, group assignments and giveaways based around that theme. A while later, this motto would be forgotten and replaced with 'entrepreneurship', a fitting ideal for the new millennium, to be coveted by every student who wanted to achieve something in life. Before these two the slogan had been 'One Earth'.

It was 1998. People still bought CDs, and they were all too familiar with the unique pain under the fingernails from trying to tear off the antitheft labels stuck to the packaging. It was also common knowledge that the batteries in a Discman always wore out before the CD playing inside it. Whenever the sisters were in the car together Viviana would use good behaviour to bribe her mother into letting her choose the radio station, which would invariably be playing 'How Bizarre' or 'Macarena'. That's right: everyone – children, teenagers and adults – listened to the radio, not only in the car but also at home; and some people, generally older ones, still listened to *Voice of Brazil* every day. Suits listened to live business news, the traffic updates during rush hour and the football on Sundays. Poorer people listened to baile funk on Imprensa FM if they were young, 98 FM if they were romantics and Copacabana if they were evangelicals. That was how you heard new music, stayed informed, felt part of a community of people who couldn't always access the remote or didn't have a second TV at home. It was important.

On that occasion the Spice Girls were playing, and Viviana was singing along quietly in the back seat of the car, symbolically holding her Discman for effect. Lucinda, who was riding in the front with their mother, said:

'I'm not going to French wearing make-up.'

'Lucy, wash your face and go.'

'But I don't know what kind of gunk they'll put on my hair, it'll be all gross… Anyway, I'll be shattered.'

Cássia almost smiled as she repeated her daughter's words:

'Shattered…'

They arrived at the studio. Cássia began to deploy her perfect parallel parking. Lucinda was tense, her body frozen stiff in her seat, her hands touching the space beneath her knees. Looking backwards as she completed the manoeuvre, Cássia said:

'OK, I've got to get to the court now. Vivi will stay with you, Lucy, and when you're done, page me. And order a cab back. No buses.'

Lucinda nodded and pressed her lips together, looking straight ahead:

'OK.'

Viviana showed no reaction. She asked for some money to buy a Mupy soya drink at the bakery opposite and was given it.

The sisters went up in the lift. In the lobby a pretty blonde girl, probably from the talent agency and already in full make-up, was sitting on a bench, awaiting her turn.

A pale, nervous-looking boy had just come out, shaking out the shirt that was glued to his thin frame.

They separated without a word, Vivi sitting in the nearest seat to the exit while Lucinda was greeted by the producer.

'Good morning,' he said, checking his clipboard. 'Lu-cin-da, right? My name's Renato, I'm the producer here at French Connection, how are you? Have you brought your signed permission form? Excellent. Wait here, please. Your name will be called soon, OK?'

Lucinda sat down, waited for a while and was called. She noticed that the foundation she was about to put on had to be taken from a bag on the top shelf of a cupboard. All the other candidates must have used the ivory colour, which was still on the table. Because of the air conditioning the cream felt cold as it made contact with her face, a pleasant sensation. Once the foundation had been applied, the thick layer of powder hid the acne marks on the lower part of her cheek. It had been far better since she'd begun using the acid cream, but the scars were still visible.

Just before she left the make-up booth, through the crack in the door Lucinda caught a glimpse of the blonde girl leaving the studio with a sad smile on her face.

Moments later, the producer came up to where Lucinda was waiting and said:

'You're next, come in. What was your name again?'

'Lucy.'

'Please come in, Lucy,' he said, placing his hand on her back and guiding her towards a door that had been painted black. They went in and the producer asked Lucinda to

11

position herself within the white square formed by masking tape on the floor. Renato spoke in a soft, soothing voice while Lucinda attempted to avoid showing any signs of nervousness.

'You need to look into the teleprompter, where the text is, see? You read straight off it, and it'll look like you're facing the camera. The text is all in French so our French teacher can assess your pronunciation' – Renato pointed towards the teacher sitting next to the camera. 'No need to rush, read slowly. We'll control the prompter, so the text will scroll as you read it. Don't move your body from side to side too much, but don't stay completely still either. That way you'll look more comfortable. Got it?'

Lucinda understood. She looked ahead, readying a half-smile.

'Ready, Lucy?'

She nodded.

From the door, he announced:

'Recording!'

While Lucinda read the text in the style of a class presentation, the producer looked through the open black door at the bench, where he saw a girl sitting alone. The last one. Then he could have lunch. He walked over to her.

'Have you come for the screen test?'

The girl looked up from the drink in her hands.

'No. I'm Viviana. Lucy's sister.'

'How old are you?'

'Thirteen,' she lied.

'Do you study French too? Want to do the test?'

Viviana kept looking at him, motionless.

'Go on, do the test,' he said, pointing to the make-up artist's door. 'Make-up's in there. You hardly need it. Go there and then straight into the studio. Wait, there's someone in there now,' he said, craning his neck. 'You're next.'

He held the clipboard out to Viviana. The permission form Cássia had signed for Lucinda was at the top.

'Please fill this in while you're waiting.'

There was a sneaky gap after Lucinda's name into which Viviana's would fit perfectly. She understood and began to write.

'I don't have an ID.'

'No worries. Leave it blank.'

With his hands in his pockets he watched her fill in the form, then checked it and escorted her to the make-up room.

In no time at all she went from the test to that photo in the Sunday supplement, which got passed around the classrooms and toilets of the school over and over until it was a crumpled mess. The New Year fashion section showed Viviana with a glass of sparkling wine in her hand, toasting a blue-eyed model with a blond centre parting, his fringe falling to the sides and forming an M shape. Inside, Viviana's brown shoulder blades were draped with a halterneck top, a single piece of glimmering cloth ending in a V shape that revealed her perfect little belly button as well as, somehow, the outline of her back. The pearlescent blouse, almost perforated by Viviana's tiny breasts, formed a sharp contrast with her skin and her hair, which had been strategically gathered and draped over her shoulder.

The same went for her brown hand with French tips resting in the gap in the boy's white shirt, just below his first undone button. His chest was also brown, but from the sun, not naturally. It was also shaved: he must have been a swimmer. Or a rent boy.

•   •   •

Now Viviana was a thirty-one-year-old woman, and she was missing. The police didn't care. As much as Lucinda feared she was the wrong person to be in charge of investigating her sister's disappearance, there was no one else. As the car approached the highway, she feared she was heading to a confrontation, but she had to try.

PART I

BEFORE

1

LUCINDA

Lucinda wakes at dawn, without needing an alarm. She watches the piercing light slip through the edges of the blackout curtain, then turns over and reaches for her phone to check the time. The system has been updated overnight and the weather forecast for the day reads thirty-three degrees.

She looks over to the other side of the bed, where Nelson is sleeping. There isn't the slightest possibility of her going back to sleep and even if there was she has to get up early today, so it wouldn't be worth the effort. She can sleep more tonight, as much as she wants, because it's Friday. She walks to the shower, removing her nightwear on the way.

On some days, such as today, she wakes kicking the air; it always happens at dawn. The anxiety leaves her legs twitching nervously. It's a long-term problem and it had got a lot better after several treatments, including dental ones. But from time to time it mysteriously shows its face again.

She isn't going to wash her hair so she ties it into a bun and covers it with a shower cap. She grabs the soap and lathers it across her body, under her armpits, beneath her breasts, on her neck, her face, before something makes her jump: it's the alarm ringing out loudly from above the sink. She reaches out her hand, dries it on the towel and slides her finger over the mobile screen. It would have gone off again in ten minutes if she hadn't gone to the effort of deactivating the whole sequence of alarms she'd programmed.

She gets dressed, eats an apple and makes some coffee. She won't wake Nelson from his jealousy-inducing deep sleep.

She heads downstairs. Ten to seven. She contemplates the traffic, which is already coming to a standstill at Jardim Botânico, and darts between the cars going down the street. Anyone who saw her would think she was very eager to spend the next fifty minutes talking about herself to an accredited professional. But she's only eager to make the appointment. Get there and be done with it.

Before entering the room she looks at the phone in her hand, aware that it's time to switch it off, which she does. She sits down on the yellow-fabric sofa and the psychologist says, 'Love the braid.'

She steadies herself so as not to reply 'What, am I more "feminine" now?' Or maybe the comment was intended as a provocation, to make her react exactly that way. She is incapable of reading that white woman with dark glasses, a few years older than her. She wonders again why she still goes. The setting, intended to be benevolent, the pastel-y tones of the decor; all of it rubs her up the wrong way.

But she needs to be good. She needs to try.

She starts talking. At least today she has a good opener.

'I'm alone in Rio today. My mother and sister are travelling. To different places.'

'For work or pleasure?'

'Well, my sister's doing some modelling somewhere – again. So I'm feeding her cat and watering her plants – again. Her apartment being near my work and all. My mother's case is different; she almost never travels. She's very focussed, a real workaholic. Her doctor forced her to take some time off. She's gone to the Caribbean with two friends. So, pleasure.'

'And what do you think about your mother's trip?'

'I think everyone needs to think about themselves from time to time. Deep down I think that's what she was trying to do, in her own way. But eventually the body gets fed up.'

It's always this way: at the beginning she doesn't feel like talking, then she warms up and embarks upon a monologue until her time is up. That's what's happening now – yet again. After the door closes behind her, Lucinda turns her mobile back on. She walks out onto the street and heads home. She eats a cereal bar. Then she gets into the car and picks the traffic jam she wants to face today: the one near Rodrigo de Freitas Lagoon or the one facing the Corcovado Mountain. Not many options towards neighbouring Humaitá.

She enters the changing room and starts wrapping her fists. She likes to think of psychoanalysis as a prelude to a beating. 'If you join the two together it's super Jungian,' she had once said, making Nelson cackle. But she's semi-serious. She needed to do things with her body for her mind to work properly, which was why she liked the two activities to be close together. So her Fridays consisted of a trip to a psychoanalyst at seven followed immediately by *muay thai*.

But does it have to be something so violent, her mother's voice asks in her head? Yes. It would seem so. Since childhood she'd tried ballet, jazz dance, street dance, Olympic gymnastics, theatre, even a short spell learning various instruments (keyboard, both electric and acoustic guitar, the bass). Lucinda should have had a hunch, given how much she always liked judo and capoeira classes at holiday camps. Now she can remember how the other, smaller kids feared her and how she feared their fear. She found it crippling. Not any more. Now they were all adults, and no one was going to call her a bulldog or dyke for doing what her body demanded. And if they did, she could beat them to a pulp.

They warm up with ropes and jogging, then the tally series, then paired fights. Lucinda's pair is the only other woman in the class, Taciana, a classic devilish blonde, even though the colour is artificial. She would almost be petite if her body were not a solid mass of protein-aided muscle. Today she's wearing a red bandana emblazoned with mini skull-and-crossbones motifs. Lucinda isn't afraid of hitting her.

She leaves the class thinking about travelling with Nelson. They could rent a cottage or a lodge in the mountains and just go. They've never done that. She takes her gloves off, picks up her bag from the small room by the tatami and walks downstairs to the women's changing rooms.

Removing her robes, she looks at herself in the mirror, sweaty and unkempt in her puffy shorts and black and pink XL sports bra. She remembers the time she watched an MMA fight free of charge because Viviana was asked to be a 'ring girl', which meant holding up the signs announcing each round. She had worn the sex shop version of the male fighters' kit: tiny, black body-hugging shorts with a little fake belt and a bikini top that lacked any real structure for her breasts, unlike the one Lucinda was removing now. Even so, Viviana had given the impression of looking a bit sweaty, or oiled-up, perhaps on the organisation's orders, and had worn her hair in a pretty French braid that was, in fact, practical for fighting. Like the one Lucinda is wearing now.

She starts undoing it. She takes shampoo, conditioner, a comb and a towel from her bag and walks into the shower. She remembers when she first began to pick up on how life doesn't treat everyone equally. Her mother, Cássia Bocayuva, was the daughter of a Maranhão notary public, the niece of a great lawyer and the cousin of several judges spread out across the country. A princess of the Brazilian legal profession. She had always been the 'Bocayuva girl', with all her male cousins, and no one found it strange when she also decided to go into that profession, although they did find it strange when she actually made up her mind to practise the law, not even considering the safest career choice for women of colour: studying hard for the civil servant exams that led to cushy, tenured judiciary jobs.

Cássia's mother had died quite young, and even though she had studied at one of the best girls' schools in Rio, which accepted this little mestizo girl after her father pulled rank, Cássia felt that the upbringing she had received at the school and from her nannies was insufficient, and she wanted her daughters to have everything she had lacked when it came to femininity. She pierced their ears when they were still babies, took Viviana and Lucinda to malls, bikini waxers and beauty salons – only the most exclusive and expensive, where the staff would praise their hair and skin before attacking them with chemicals, then once again before producing the bill. There were also trips to beaches, mushy romantic movies, music and language lessons, and volleyball – no other ball sports were allowed. It was the tried-and-tested way of becoming a woman, at least in the Rio de Janeiro of the time.

One day, a fourteen-year-old Lucinda came home with an eyebrow piercing. Cássia's reaction was very different from what the girl had been expecting: instead of shouting at her or criticising her, she simply looked unperturbed. Her expression read: *So smart… and yet she understands nothing. Such a shame.* That was when Lucinda understood everything.

Previously Lucinda had thought that her mother's plan was for her daughters to climb the social ladder in a way that she had never managed – becoming the most beautiful, the most popular and the coolest, until eventually they nabbed the most coveted matches and produced grandchildren. Femininity was a competitive sport, even between sisters. This was something Lucinda abhorred, with her 90s girl-power integrity and the excess weight she carried, which had the effect of covertly sidelining her from the game. In reality, the game was never meant to be played by these specific women. The three Bocayuvas had mestizo faces, dark copper skin and straight hair that fell like curtains over their faces. Lucinda was the only one to have inherited a certain waviness from her father, and spent a huge amount of time submitting herself to hydrations and relaxations to rein it in. The game being played by both sisters was that of appearing normal – in other words, white – just like almost everyone else at their school. Clearly, getting piercings didn't help that. Even if it was just a silver stud, it wasn't the same thing as her blonde classmate who had six hoops in her ears, as well as an extra one in her nose. Of course, when you're a Barbie you can do what you like.

Lucinda gets out of the shower and, still naked, leans over to grab her mobile from the outside pocket of her rucksack. She unlocks it and stares at it, incredulous. It's a photo. A photo someone has taken of their own erect cock, with her phone, while she was still in the class. A protrusion of yellowy-beige skin skewing to the left and a foot inside a brown leather shoe below it, standing on the dirty-white tiles in the room where everyone leaves their things. Lucinda had been the first to get there after the instructor.

She tries to recognise the footwear. Who was wearing leather shoes today? No one who actually works at the gym. Maybe someone else from the class. In her head she goes over all the unremarkable men she fights two or three times a week. She studies the yellowy and darkened regions across the body of the penis, suggesting an owner with skin of a similar colour. Pedro's is pinky-white, Dênis's a dark shade of black, Rafael's brownish like hers. They were all eliminated. In terms of people with that shade of skin there was that boring lawyer... what was his name again? Régis. He could be the exhibitionist, except he always wears dark bottoms, and in the photo you can see a beige hemline over the brown shoe. Beige trousers and brown shoes is the outfit of someone who works in admin, or a public servant. As Lucinda sits down on the toilet seat and pulls her leggings on, she goes through names and faces in her head. Bruno. Telmo. Cristiano. Maurício.

The nutsack isn't visible in the photo, Lucinda thinks, slowly raising her arms to do up her bra and then quickly lowering one of them to touch the screen so that it stays lit. If the balls were in the photo, looking at how wrinkled they were and how low they drooped could give away the age of the perpetrator, in which case she would accuse Cristiano, the only member of the class approaching sixty. Truthfully, though, he's the least likely of the remaining suspects, because he probably wouldn't know the trick of unlocking a phone by sliding up the camera icon, and besides, he wouldn't be able to get a hard-on just like that, under pressure and on demand. She feels bad about thinking this atrocious chain of thoughts about her classmates. But that's what it is, right? Exhibitionism. A crime in which the culprit wants to be discovered. And admired... for his virility, his ingenuity and his *courage*. Worse of all – it dawns on Lucinda – she's doing exactly what he wants: trying to discover his identity. Perhaps even go after him.

As soon as she has this thought, she knows who it is: Bruno. Her neighbour. Of course. All those tubs of whey he is regularly seen removing from his car outside the building they both inhabit… and the obsession with body image – Bruno practised more than one martial art – and the indignation he must have felt at his chubby neighbour seeming uninterested in him, even when she was kicking him and throwing him to the floor. She didn't know what she was missing out on… obviously. Lucinda feels a little disappointed with herself, annoyed at not having thought of him in the first place.

In her head Lucinda sees the car boot, the whey and a blonde woman walking around the car – girlfriend, wife, beach bimbo or the pretty white girl from the office, she doesn't know and doesn't care. The car belongs to her; so does the whey and the dick. If Lucinda wants, she can have a bit of that too. The image of degradation is complete.

She's so distracted by the surprise dick she almost loses track of the time. She arrives at the studio panting and immediately starts helping the intern adjust the reflector before going over any items left on her to-do list and hurrying the guest through the corridor. Like all the programmes they shoot, this one is educational: an interview with software developers on the role of schools and universities in their work (unsurprisingly it had been extremely difficult to find anyone). When she's finally let out for lunch, she notices there are six missed calls on her mobile. Number not recognised, São Paulo code. Must be telemarketing. She checks her notifications, likes a few posts and puts the device back in her bag.

She looks at the wall clock and discovers that she's eaten lunch at eleven a.m., even earlier than usual. Public service does have its advantages, she thinks: although the blocks of time vary, the routine is more or less the same, and the lunch hour is actually an hour. It's important to chew slowly, not just gulp the food down: that's what causes the damage. She opens a packaged salad-in-a-cup while the warm part of her meal revolves in the microwave. She was a regular customer – addict would be more accurate – at the ten-real salad stand at a certain health food store, because it was the only way to force herself to eat right, given her non-stop lifestyle.

'Crazy salad', the label reads. Lucinda pours half the dressing over the leafy top layer and plunges the fork in to bring up the most interesting part from the bottom: shredded chicken, palm hearts and peas. She pours out the other half of the dressing, tosses the salad a little longer and starts to eat. She notices that her colleague Diane is eating a healthy-looking dish from a square Tupperware, consisting of okra, hummus and aubergine. Diane doesn't like hot food. As soon as she's finished, her colleague excuses herself and goes over to the window to smoke while Lucinda, after finishing her salad, begins cutting up her sad-looking chicken cannelloni and inserting pieces of it into her mouth.

'Are you going to Marlene's party, Cindy?' Diane asks.

'No, I never pitched in,' Lucinda replies.

'The third-floor team are super chilled.'

Lucinda looks askance at Diane and stops eating.

'Not with me they aren't, Di.'

'What? The thing about the dress code?'

'They called you Elsa and me Moana.'

'That was just Silvia. The rest of them are cool. Running away isn't the solution.'

'Maybe it isn't, but I've had enough.'

'Come with me,' puffs Diane. 'If they tease you, I'll tear their heads off.'

Lucinda chuckles.

'I'll think about it.'

As she washes her cutlery, Lucinda dwells on her notorious work nickname. As soon as the Disney film came out, people took to calling her Moana – to go with her blonde friend Diana, aka Elsa – and they made sure she knew it. The character was cute; the nickname, not so much. By using it her colleagues were saying: *We see your difference, honey.* There was also a hint of something sensual in the way they had turned a children's character into a non-compliment that was essentially sexual in nature. It was like when Viviana had got called Tainá at school, around the time that film about the little Indigenous girl had come out. Lucinda hadn't received this kind of nickname before; hers had always been openly insulting. She had had to wait until chubby child characters with naturally wavy hair became conceivable in pop culture to even be considered. Even then, she wasn't happy about it.

Lucinda finishes eating and goes back to work. It's desk work now, in front of a screen. As she sits down she feels her phone vibrate. She's received a message, from the same São Paulo number. Telemarketing people don't usually leave messages, as far as she knows. Intrigued, she presses play.

'Lucinda? You OK? This is Graziane, I'm a friend of your sister's, from São Paulo. Sorry to have called you so many times, but I'm kind of worried. Viviana and I had agreed to meet today and she hasn't shown up. Do you know if she's OK? Did she end up going back to Rio?'

Lucinda listens to the message again. The girl has a Paraná accent. She imagines a statuesque blonde, Eastern European origin. A model like Viviana. And with a name like that she must be from the country. Another message comes.

'She hasn't responded to any of my messages, not even to show that she's read them, since last night. I'm worried. Let me know if you manage to get through to her.'

Could this be a trick? Some new scam? Lucinda decides to call her sister right away. She doesn't pick up. Lucinda's heart starts beating faster.

She sends text messages. She calls Viviana's landline until it stops ringing. She calls her sister's mobile nine times, and each time it goes straight to answerphone. As she leaves a message on Vivi's voicemail she rushes to the disabled toilet on the third floor, gulping in huge mouthfuls of air before expelling them immediately. She bumps into Diane on the back stairs, smoking. She stubs out the cigarette on the floor with her shoe and grabs her shoulder.

'My God, you've gone green,' Diane comments, touching Lucinda's arm.

Her hand is warm and dry as sandpaper. Lucinda continues to walk down the stairs, expels an 'I feel sick', pushes open the fire escape doors on the next floor down, shuts herself in the toilet and closes her eyes. No one will look for her there. It's been a while since she had an attack of this kind, she thinks, touching her sternum to calm herself down – my God, it's been years. But this one doesn't feel like the earlier ones, which had no obvious trigger; this time the reason is entirely clear. She opens her bag and searches around for anything that might help her, medication, her diary, a notebook. As the objects fall to the floor one by one, the word PREMONITION appears in her head, written in a silver speech bubble, as if her brain needed to spell the thing out to make it real. Premonitions aren't real, she thinks, but what is it? What *was* it?

Here's what it is: Lucinda is certain Viviana has disappeared, *really* disappeared, that her lack of contact isn't just a coincidence. She had left on Monday and planned to be back on Friday afternoon; over the four days of her sister's absence, Lucinda only had to go to her apartment twice, that's what they'd agreed. Yesterday, since feeding the cat and going home to sleep, she hadn't communicated with her sister, not even to wish her a safe journey. Josefel and the plants don't need another visit yet; they can go forty-eight hours without supervision. But today there are no notifications showing she's read the messages, none of her calls have been answered, there isn't a trace of Viviana at her place and she hasn't sent a message saying she's been held up. Something's wrong. Something's happened to her.

'Something.' She's dead of course. In a ditch somewhere.

Now she, the big sister, total dope, always on the run, always exhausted, must quiet her mind and think. Where had Viviana actually gone? She doesn't even know. She didn't bother to ask, since her sister travelled so often. Vivi might have gone to do some modelling in the south, perhaps in Curitiba, where the agency tended to find more work for her. But this Graziane – a friend Lucinda had never heard of – had called from São Paulo, that was where they were meant to meet...

She keeps frantically calling Viviana, checking to see if the two grey ticks for delivered or the two blue ones for seen appear next to her sent messages. But no matter how many times she looks, they don't. Her sister and her phone are inseparable. If it had been stolen she'd have got a new one in the blink of an eye.

She checks Viviana's social media accounts. No recent posts. Viviana has an Instagram portfolio full of publicity spots, photos taken between shoots, making-ofs from films, adverts and series she'd had roles in and lots of photos of her in a white T-shirt or bikini. Lucinda has never liked that account and now, looking at it in detail, she understands why: the mixture of private and public, intended to create a fake sense of intimacy. The so-called private life was just a stunt, anyway: look at her, smiling as she drinks her açai smoothie, the perfect Rio girl, mistress of the sun and the sand, wearing a yellow bikini from some designer beachwear company's summer pre-collection. Californian highlights in her black hair. Legs for miles. No one could ever tell from this that Viviana didn't actually like beaches. Or smiling. Lucinda glances at the high number of followers, which for all she knows could have been paid for. Most recent post: two days ago, wearing a long dress, in a studio with an infinite white background, location unnamed.

She calls the reception at Vivi's São Paulo apartment and talks to a porter called Sérgio, who says the last time she was there was the afternoon of the previous day. She calls the friend in São Paulo.

'Hey, Graziane, this is Lucinda, Viviana's sister. Unfortunately, I still haven't heard from her. What had you arranged for today?'

'Brunch.'

'When did you last speak?'

'Yesterday afternoon. To arrange brunch.'

'How do you know each other?'

'We're both models.'

'Right.' Lucinda is satisfied for now. 'Sorry for the interrogation, OK? I'm just worried because I can't get through to her either.' She is, it's true, but she mainly asked to find out exactly who she was dealing with. 'Have you any idea where she could have got to?'

'No, none.'

Is she lying? Hiding something? Lucinda decides to press her.

'No idea at all? Have a think.'

'She did mention a job on the horizon, but, look, it was on the side. Better you don't mention it to the agency.'

'She didn't say what it was?'

'No.'

'All right. I think I'll talk to the police here. Could you try and find a lead there, call some hospitals…? I'll call some hospitals too. Keep me informed?'

'Of course.'

Lucinda says goodbye with an utterly insincere 'Stay calm. We'll find Vivi.' She feels her head spinning. Viviana, vanished. And her idiot sister, who only found out from a stranger. Viviana could have been in an accident, lying unconscious in some shabby São Paulo hospital. Or someone could have done something bad to her. Some crazy guy who was in love with her, or a jealous colleague. Who knows, maybe Graziane.

Lucinda looks at her tiny round photo in the messenger app, a medium shot with a natural background. She is indeed blonde, statuesque, Eastern European-looking. A nymph. She can't imagine a woman like that being dangerous, except in a film noir. Perhaps that was her appeal.

She begins calling hospitals, giving Viviana's name and describing her appearance. She also calls some hospitals in São Paulo, and then some morgues in the centre and outskirts. None of them have seen Viviana. 'She's a model, thin, tall, over six foot. Dark skin, Indigenous features.' It wasn't hard to be sure no one meeting that description had been in any of those places since last night.

Her sister was nowhere to be seen.

She calls her mother. It goes straight to voicemail. Of course, she is in the middle of her long-overdue holiday.

As far back as she can remember, Cássia has always been busy. After the separation she'd decided to open her own practice, finally leaving the one owned by her father's old friend, who had refused to make her a member even though he had no heirs at the business or any other employee more dedicated than her. Bocayuva & Associates set out to operate in the field of tax law but it was in family law, with the boom in divorces and the subsequent battles over child custody, that Cássia's practice had been propelled to the kind of low-key fame so many lawyers covet. Her ex-classmates at the elite schools were getting divorced, and they all went to her.

From her many years as a tax lawyer, Cássia knew all the tricks for hiding money abroad; at the same time, because she was a woman starting her own business, no one paid her any attention. They didn't know what she was capable of. She signed many extrajudicial agreements with future ex-husbands simply by threatening to take information she had acquired to Inland Revenue. These successful cases allowed her to expand, and she began recruiting talent, young and old, until she'd built up a robust and widely respected practice. Nothing had disappointed her more than neither one of her daughters wanting to study law and continue down the path she had so triumphantly ploughed for them.

Lucinda doesn't leave a message on her mother's voice-mail because she knows she doesn't check it. Cássia's date of birth means that she is a cross between a young baby boomer and a pioneer Generation-Xer. She is a real control freak; she adores her phone but at the same time she is exhausted by all that new, rapidly changing technology. Dealing with all kinds of people and issues through that incredibly versatile device, Cássia avoids calls, neglects her voicemail, ignores emails, takes days to check messages (if ever), and her secretary has become highly skilled at filtering calls to the office landline, only communicating the most important messages to her. By the time this is happening Lucinda and Viviana are grown-up, healthy and moving on in life so Cássia assumes they don't need much urgent attention. Her health, however, has begun to suffer from her non-stop lifestyle, and after her most recent check-up the doctor prescribed a proper holiday.

Lucinda tries her mother again. When she hears the automated voice she wonders if it's worth risking leaving a message. But what would she say? *Hey Mum, you OK? Viviana's been missing since yesterday, according to her acquaintance who I've never heard of before, and definitely since lunchtime by my watch. I still haven't attempted to find out where she's been over the last few days, and I haven't gone to the police, but I have called all the local hospitals and morgues, and nothing. Basically, we both know she's been dumped in some filthy river somewhere.*

Lucinda predicts that Cássia's reaction would fluctuate between two, non-mutually exclusive poles: frantic diligence and criticism of her negligence as an older sister. In order to demonstrate her dedication and presence of mind Lucinda would need to take some action, preferably several actions; at the very least, she would need to discover her sister's last known location, gather possible clues concerning her disappearance and deal with the police. And she'd have to do all of that before Cássia heard her message and got back to her. Make some effort to play the part of older sister. Then she'd be ready to face her mother. Even so, she knew that whatever happened she would be faced with her mother's wild and uncontainable fury, as if she had personally led her younger sister by the

34

hand into a forest and left her there without so much as a breadcrumb to keep her going.

Because of this, Lucinda chooses to leave a laconic message on her mother's voicemail and a text message on all the chat apps: 'Hey Mum, I can't get through to Viviana, I'm looking for her, call me as soon as you can.' She takes a deep breath and commands her own genes to do their best Cássia. There must be one in there somewhere.

2

LUCINDA

After looking unsuccessfully for a space on Bambina Street, Lucinda parks in one of the streets by the mall. Driving through Botafogo was hell, but it's the nearest police station and she has no time to lose. She checks her mobile: maybe her sister or her mother has seen the messages by now. No. Despite the heat she puts the blazer on; perhaps it will make her look more respectable.

The police station is in an old, pastel-toned house. Next to the wooden counter a young couple waiting for their report to be printed are asking the attending officer, a man with thick glasses and a white ponytail, some final questions. Their car has been stolen. Wringing her fingers, Lucinda awaits her turn as she gazes at the Map of Recent Thefts and Muggings in Botafogo and Environs stuck to the wall. The couple take their report and leave the station.

'Yes?'

'I want to report a missing person. My sister.'

'How long has she been missing?'

'A day.'

'Twenty-four hours?'

'No… twenty hours.'

'Where did she go missing?'

'In São Paulo. She lives here, though; she was away for work. I was looking after her cat, and suddenly she stopped answering my messages. She hasn't even seen them.'

The man peers at her over his glasses, unperturbed:

'Are you sure she's missing? Couldn't she just have lost her phone?'

'I'm certain. A friend of hers called, asking about her. They'd arranged to meet, but my sister didn't show up. The porter at her building in São Paulo hasn't seen her since yesterday either.'

'Look, ideally you should file the report in São Paulo. Is there no way she could simply be flying, or maybe her phone has run out of battery? She could have lost her charger or...'

'But she should have been back in Rio by now.'

'And she hasn't come back.'

'No.'

'If you're sure,' the attendant says, looking at her askance, 'you can file a report. Just remember it's a crime to alert the police unnecessarily.'

Lucinda is beginning to get annoyed.

'Yes, I'm sure. Go ahead and open the case.'

Place of disappearance? São Paulo. Full name? Viviana Bocayuva dos Santos. Date of birth? 22nd January 1987. Profession? Model. Marital status? Single. Boyfriend? No. Any mental disturbances or problems? No. Does she take drugs? No! Place of residence? Humaitá.

The receptionist prints a form and says: 'Check and sign.' She signs.

'Now what happens?'

'The case goes to the Missing Persons Unit. They'll look for your sister in the hospitals and morgues. But it would be a good idea to contact all your relatives, she could be with any of them.'

'OK.'

He hands her a bit of paper that's been cut with a ruler and circles a number at the top.

'That's the number for the Missing Persons Unit. If you or they find any information regarding your sister, you can use it to communicate. Send a recent photo of her to the WhatsApp. They'll make a digital poster and share it on Facebook. If possible, do a post on social media, you never know, someone might know something.'

Lucinda puts the papers in her bag and leaves the station. Outside, a truck full of military police brandishing rifles is pulling in. A black boy, shaven-headed and shirtless, sits in the barred back seat, his hands cuffed behind him and his head lowered.

As she walks out she removes her sweaty blazer. She quickly manoeuvres her car out of the space and goes straight to Vivi's house in Humaitá. She drives without paying much attention on the journey and almost without formulating any coherent thoughts: *Evening appointment, evening appointment… I'll look at her laptop and find out where she's gone, I know it's invasive but I need to.* It's a miracle that she doesn't crash the car, or else pure reflex. As she takes the lift up to her sister's apartment the panic attack rears its head once more. By the time she gets to the front door she's dripping with sweat and her heart is pounding. She opens the door, sees the cat in the room and goes straight to the computer.

On the coffee table the laptop looks more like a butcher's block. Lucinda perches on the edge of the sofa, opens it and turns it on. The screen asks for a password. She tries 'Viviana'. 'Vivi'. 'Lucinda'. 'Cássia'. 'RitadeCássia', her mother's first name that she never uses, in upper case, lower case, upper and lower, no accents. She tries 'Josefel', the cat's name. She combines each one with dates of birth. Nothing. Shit. She has that horrible sensation again. The thought seeping in through the barricades she has put up: *trying to find out if your sister is dead or not.* Eventually she'll find her. Dead. Lucinda realises she's started to pace up and down the room, looking at her sister's books and belongings, searching for inspiration, any clue. Too many books, ceiling-level shelves full of them (and even more in the guest room). There's no way she'd ever be able to single out a reference from one of these books that might help her guess the password. She's wasting time. *Why the hell can't she use obvious passwords or write them down on an eraser like everyone else?* Maybe there was a Post-it somewhere, a bit of paper with the password written on it. She goes over to the pad by the phone. She remembers people scrawling on them in films with a tilted pencil, in an attempt to make out what had been written more forcefully in pen on the top sheet. But she knows Viviana is way too organised to leave so much as a slip of paper out of place. In addition, she almost never uses the landline. Nor, strangely, is she a fan of leaving anything on the cloud or letting any apps know your location – she claims not to trust these supposedly secure services, especially the American ones. She's pretty paranoid. Still, though, she could have written these important things down somewhere, in case of emergency. A place her family members would be able to find.

Well. Maybe.

Lucinda enters the bedroom, opens the cupboard, pushes the hangers apart in one go, an equal number on either side, and looks down. At the bottom is a safe where Viviana keeps jewellery and money. Lucinda knows the combination. She tries twice, her hand trembling. Envelopes stuffed with cash, euros and dollars, as well as way too many jewels for someone who can never wear them in this violent city. She pulls out handfuls, placing them on the bed and illuminating the base of the safe with her phone's torch. She opens the envelopes, the boxes, leafs through the wads of cash. No passwords. Not there.

Then she starts going through the drawers like the mother of a teenager. She finds vibrators, sexy lingerie. She pushes the drawers and they glide shut. Above the hangers there is a shelf with an enormous pile of individually wrapped manga comics. Lucinda pulls one of the towers of comics out and behind it sees only more and more mounds of paper. She shouts and hits the sliding doors. *Where the fuck is the password? I haven't got time for games. When are you going to emerge, Vivi? Appear*, she orders her. *Come on. Now. Call me now so I can be beside myself with anger but ultimately relieved.* Lucinda looks at her phone screen. *Call. Call now. Stop messing around.* She flops onto the bed with her eyes closed and tries to calm her fits of tears. After some time taking deep breaths she dials her sister's number again and watches one more futile call fall into the void. That zen shit never works for her, she thinks: she needs something pharmaceutical.

Lucinda leaps off the bed and throws open the bathroom cupboard. At the back, behind a wide selection of creams and beauty treatments is a storage box with bottles and pouches full of leaves and flowers and a smaller one with ointments and pills, some of them with a black strip to show that they are controlled substances. She swallows one, a tranquilliser – no need for water. She rummages through the bigger box and finds a heap of herbs and mushrooms, all medicinal in one way or another. She remembers how years ago her sister, before she went to live abroad, had suggested she microdose mushrooms to combat her depression symptoms – it had worked for her. Lucinda is tempted to leave everything as it is, but she ends up putting each thing back in its correct place in the wardrobe. All of a sudden, as she stands there, an idea comes straight to her.

Sitting down at the computer, Lucinda clicks on the *forgot your password?* option. *See hint*, the screen offers. Lucinda accepts.

The hint is: HE COMES FLYING IN FROM WHERE YOU LEAST EXPECT.

As if they were a separate entity, her fingers type a password she had once created for an account she'd shared with her sister. The screen blinks and welcomes her in. Lucinda exhales all the air that had been imprisoned in her lungs.

The password was 'Tesserascinus', with an at symbol in place of the a and the number 5 in place of the Ss.

Tesseract + fascinus, the ancient Roman symbol of the winged phallus. She remembers telling her sister the password she'd chosen, Viviana's slow, guttural laughter and the way she'd thrown her head back, in full approval of her sister's creation. The sisters had the same linguistic–visual sense of humour: the idea of a cosmic fascinus, a four-dimensional being, coming to get you from an angle which you, a being limited to three dimensions, could not even see, was monstrously irresistible.

First she scans the tabs already open in the browser. Her email is full of spam and old work offers, all read – up until the end of the previous day. A message from the airline informing Vivi that she could now check in for her flight, and another one, unread, from this morning, reminding her that she still hadn't checked in. Lucinda clicks on the Sent folder. From what she can see her sister doesn't often send emails. Or receive them. Confirmations of attendance at events and shops informing her that products were being dispatched were the most frequent. Among Viviana's purchases, Lucinda recognises the name of an online sex shop from which she has also purchased items. She doesn't look at the content. Instead, she opens one of several emails from the sender easyinvest.com, this one informing her of an asset suddenly plummeting in value. A password is required for further information. She tries a few before admitting defeat.

She goes to the Facebook tab displaying the 'Viviana Bocayuva' fanpage. She is described in English as a *Brazilian actress and model*, a relic of the now-distant period Viviana spent living abroad. The wall functions as a space for self-promotion and is closed to visitor posts from fans. But the message inbox is overflowing. Women asking if she was the girl from the gym app or the flyer for the burger place, asking for tips about slimming or how to get started in the profession; lots of men telling her she's beautiful, one calling her ugly. Someone who claimed to be a photographer offering her a free book, as if she was fourteen years old and had no career. Viviana hardly ever replies, especially to the men.

She also roots around the messages on her personal Facebook profile – more men calling her beautiful. The most recent message is from the day before, a young guy from Curitiba saying he'd seen her on Tinder and that he thought she was beautiful, and as she hadn't swiped right on his picture he had decided to write to her on here. Viviana hadn't responded. So she really had been in Curitiba. Hmm.

Lucinda, who, like almost everyone she knows, has done some digging on other people before, remembers that from the email inbox you can access information and services linked to that account, like photos and documents kept on the cloud. She decides to investigate Viviana's recent movements.

However, going through photos, documents, detailed itineraries and synchronised contracts, she finds nothing revealing. She can only see a strange pattern in them – gaps in the calendar, photos few and far between – as if her sister's digital presence were in some way wanting. Maybe Vivi had made a tremendous effort to maintain her privacy, ticking all those well-hidden boxes that prohibit tech companies from mining and selling your data. For sure. If Viviana is so paranoid with her data and doesn't trust the cloud, where could she be keeping the essentials? Maybe on her own computer.

The Documents folder contains many text files and some spreadsheets. Lucinda double-clicks on a spreadsheet with the title AA CLIENTS. This is what she sees when it opens:

NAME	SOURCE	NOTES	DATES	LOCATIONS
Mark G.	Traveluv. com	tight but regular. Sharp teeth.	Almost every week (from Dec.)	Rio, SP
Luiz Antonio B.	Patrocina. com.br	daddy dom, always checks if using gifts (wear pink 212 and bracelet)	25/02, 03/03, 15/03, 29/03, 10/04, 23/04, 2/05, 3/06, 25/06, 2/7, 5/08, 18/08, 21/09, 01/10, 15/10	Curitiba, SP
Brazilian Couple (A and H)	3match. com	sweet, discretion needed	(12/05, 17/06 and 30/06) x3	Brasília and Rio
Benício (judge)	Andreza	bore. Smokes cigars	25/01, 3/10, 20/11	Rio
Ambroise and Denis (consulate)	Booker (c) 0	Kind, discreet, recommended me for nice gigs (poor personal hygiene!)	26/01, 06/03, 27/03, 20/04 (see referrals)	Rio
Bassam T.	Bar in Dubai	Good guy, long term client, gf, generous, dollar	Since 2010, every year	SP and Rio
Davi (agroboy)	Andreza	Pushy, big dick	15/09	Rio

Lucinda feels her heart breaking in two, splitting down the middle. That suspicion, always there, hovering, lying in wait, muffled, has just been confirmed. Definitively. There's no way back.

Shit. It makes sense. It makes huge, devastating sense. How could you not expect this given Viviana's ostentatious lifestyle? There's no way you could keep an apartment in São Paulo and another in Rio just with the money from those exhausting, poorly paid fashion shoots. The Rio one belonged to the family but it had running costs. Then there were her clothes and the innumerable beauty treatments.

Her sister… a prostitute. Lucinda forces herself to admit it. She's finally losing her innocence – at thirty-five. She finds it strange that the panic isn't coming back now, but perhaps the shock is too great.

She gets up from the sofa, covering her mouth with her hands, trying to accommodate her sister, who decided to turn herself into a product aimed at the client's total satisfaction, within her self-image as an open-minded woman. She was the optimum product, attentive, professional; she even used spreadsheets. The thing is, she didn't need to do any of this, she was so intelligent! She could do so many things. She *shouldn't* have chosen this option. And open-minded Lucinda *shouldn't* be thinking that her sister *shouldn't* do a thing. *You understand nothing, Lucinda,* as her mother had said to her when she found out about the piercing.

How did she not realise before? When had it started? She thinks back to her sister's puberty, their puberty. Lucinda fifteen, Vivi eleven, crazy about anime and X-Men.

Axé music was big. Carnival, even for Rio residents, had begun to mean a trip to Salvador, Porto de Galinhas, Porto Seguro, Trancoso – resorts gradually became the focus, but initially it was Salvador, with *abadás* and viewing boxes. Being stuck in Rio as a teenager was the worst, you were always faced with the same old dire choice: either spend the night on some dirty cement stands watching the Grupo Especial go by or head to a street party full of drunken old men molesting underage girls.

When the first opportunity to escape, in modest instalments that even the less well-off could afford, presented itself in the form of a pamphlet given out at the end of a school year, Lucinda initially hesitated. Hadn't she already been to those places with her family? But then she realised that going with a school party was different and, moreover, essential: the whole point was to strengthen bonds by committing small acts of transgression as a group. Cássia agreed and paid up, thinking that this was an excellent programme for her scruffy outcast of an eldest daughter. It would be one more step towards her social integration. Without asking, Lucinda was given two fluorescent high-waisted bikinis, that season's models, which hid her belly and brought out her natural brownness. Despite the care her mother took, something didn't go right on the trip and Lucinda came back different, more determined than ever to choose the kinds of music, people and haunts she associated with. Instead of coming back and demanding an exchange trip during the holidays in July, as Cássia might have hoped, Lucinda became a regular at Garage Club and acquired her first pair of black XL jeans.

Sometime after her debut as a model and an actress in commercials, Viviana also had her carnival trip with friends. At sixteen she spent the summer in Porto Seguro. But the trip did not, as hoped, consolidate her female friendships, largely because when she got back she continued to do the same things she had done away from Rio, without feeling the need to leave them to one side, as mere carnival adventures. This put off many of her classmates, who were more attracted to normativity and didn't like to be gossiped about, not to mention her disagreeable lack of adherence to the group, which signalled that Viviana liked to immerse herself in danger – not simply flirt with it – with older men and suburban youths. She became somewhat isolated and started hanging around with other outcasts, with whom she sometimes got into fights inspired by jealousy. Some nights she'd end up at Garage with Lucinda, which made Lucinda fully aware of just how much a model's body alters the pattern of male attention, even in alternative circles.

They fought amongst themselves too. At the time Lucinda had the impression that her sister was mostly messing around rather than having sex, at least when she was around. By then she knew that both she and her younger sister were bisexual, although the ratio between her being called a dyke and actually going with other girls was incredibly skewed owing to her body type (and, in Vivi's opinion, because Lucinda wore Nauru sneakers too often). Cássia had apparently ceased to impose any limits at all on their freedom – deep down, this was perhaps because she feared being too controlling and ending up having the two sisters stuck at home with no Cinderella to make up for it. Aside from that, she didn't have the time: since she'd opened her own practice she was always either busy working or exhausted after it.

As soon as she turned eighteen, Vivi appeared in a beer commercial, as part of a crowd of women in bikinis; the contract included an invite to the Sapucaí viewing box and other summer events around Brazil, and though attendance was compulsory anyway she enthusiastically fulfilled this clause, even managing to appear in some of the gossip magazines because she hung around with the right people.

Shortly after, their grandfather died. The Bocayuvas lost the huge, automatic income from the notary's office he had run for decades, which meant the three of them were suddenly plunged into the middle class. Lucinda applied for the civil service exams. Cássia continued to strive for her firm's ascension. With Viviana, however, it was another story.

She had barely turned twenty-one when her sources of more prestigious and well-paid work began drying up. Viviana was now only good for beach fashion, stock images, playing the mestizo woman in political adverts or else playing the role of a fitness nut, with a gleaming white smile from the dentist. Sometimes a test run as a bride or modelling winter clothes, when the advertising agency had decided to take a bet on a dark-skinned model with Kardashianised eyebrows. Never again would she be a catwalk model or fashion supplement exclusive or appear on the cover of magazines. These positions were taken by whiter, younger girls, lauded for their French features and delicate skin.

Later, when her Indigenous features began to denote diversity, demand for Viviana grew high again, but by then she was already a little old for the 'industry', as they say. Now, at thirty-one, she was already receiving offers for the part of the young non-white mother.

Lucinda realised that at times Viviana, beneath her layer of thick skin, had felt hurt by the way she had been discarded so prematurely, as well as being ostracised as a teenager. She had been accustomed to high levels of consumption since early childhood, varnished by a layer of sociopathic friendliness and armed with useful underworld contacts: Lucinda used to think that these had been the determining factors behind her sister's decision to live abroad. In fact, they had been the perfect set of prerequisites for Viviana doing something quite different: going on the game. That much was certain.

And neither Lucinda nor Cássia ever caught on to this. Questioned Viviana. Exercised any form of pressure. Perhaps they even closed their eyes to it, just as Lucinda is literally doing now, forcefully trying to wipe this day from her existence. Everything, absolutely everything has gone wrong from the moment the sun rose. She wipes her sweaty face and runs her hand through her tied-up hair, then breathes for a few moments into cupped hands. The spreadsheet is still there, calling out to her, challenging her.

Lucinda likes to read science books, about astrophysics and neurology. She knows that this horrible feeling is the brain refusing to accept reality, trying to cling to any shred of evidence that will protect her from the cruel truth. The only way out is to force it to continue. Walk hand in hand with it, step by step, until there's no solution but to gulp down every last drop.

She decides to research some of the sites on the spreadsheet, so types the name of the first one into the search bar and presses enter, wanting to believe in another explanation, in some redemption for Viviana.

Some of the sites on the spreadsheet are more explicit, with names like 'luxury escorts' and 'vip girls', which she visits but lacks the courage to scroll down. There are also regular meet-up apps, which Lucinda is aware of and imagines could have been used to scout for prospective clients, since on all the ones she accesses on the browser, the 'missvivian' account is either suspended or has almost no activity.

Traveluv.com is a travel dating site, where the client can pay you to 'accompany' them on their travels. You sign up either as a sponsor or to be sponsored.

Patrocina.com.br is similar but defines itself as a website for remunerated relationships, referring to the participants as 'daddys', 'mommys' and 'babys', with the plurals done in the Portuguese style. They both mention 'lifestyle', as does the third, 3match, which is aimed at couples 'looking for a third person for company or maybe something more.'

Company. 'Daddys'. Lifestyle. Viviana operates in the between space, the space opened up by technology and language. If you ran into trouble, all you had to do was change site or use a different term. But none of that alters her sister's true profession. There is no avoiding it. This is what her sister does for money – real money.

How would their mother react? With a cocktail of guilt for having failed irreversibly. Failed by raising her daughters in a rather neglectful way, because she'd been permissive and 'prioritised her career', leaving the two of them to their own devices. Lucinda, as the older sister, would doubtless be blamed by her mother. For Viviana's disappearance and for her being a prostitute. *Where were you when this happened?*

She starts to feel the artificial calm of the pill descend upon her rampant anxiety. A lid on a boiling pan. She goes back into the bathroom, grabs the rest of the strip and puts it in her bag. She's going to need it.

She goes back over what she knows so far. Viviana went to Curitiba (probably to see a client), then to São Paulo, organised a brunch with this friend, Graziane (whom Lucinda trusts less and less), which she did not attend, and then disappeared, perhaps at the hands of a client. The encounter in São Paulo must have been arranged over the phone. Lucinda returns to the spreadsheet and the column of phone numbers. The first belongs to a woman called Andreza, likely a colleague in the profession. What will happen if she calls her?

She figures that there must be some solidarity among hookers, a support network. As this probable colleague of Viviana's appears more than once in the Source column of the spreadsheet, it's likely that she procures clients for Vivi and perhaps also that she is close to her. Maybe she'll sympathise with the situation and tell her something useful. Lucinda is afraid she's being extremely naïve but calls anyway.

'Hello.' Husky, sensual voice. Cautious.

'Andreza?'

Longer pause than normal. You can hear the surprise coming from the woman on the other end of the line.

'Who's asking?'

'This is Lucinda, Viviana's sister.' Now Lucinda is certain. 'Is this Graziane?'

Tense silence. No confirmation. Lucinda proceeds.

'I know everything, don't worry. I just want to find Vivi.'

'Oh, I wasn't going to tell.'

'You could have told me straight away.'

'She doesn't want the family to know. It's not the kind of thing you talk to the police about...'

'I didn't. I've just found out, after opening her computer just now. I saw the spreadsheet. Do you work together?'

'We do.'

'Friend?'

'More than friend. I don't know if this is shocking to you...'

'No.'

'I'm looking for her. I'm in a taxi right now to track down someone who might have something to do with it. Or might not.'

'Who?'

'An ex of hers, photographer. Wait a minute: you managed to get into her computer. Did you see her location?'

'I tried, but there's nothing in the browser; she hasn't given permission.'

'Vivi has another mobile and another email address. Find that email account on the computer and see if she's logged in. I know she turns on the location services on this one. For safety. She shares it with me, but only in real time, and her dot hasn't come on since this morning. On the computer you'll be able to see her complete movements.'

Lucinda asks her to wait a moment, leaves the mobile on speaker, looks for another logged-in email on the browser, finds another of Viviana's addresses and confirms that the location services are activated. There's a record of all the locations her sister visited up until seven the previous evening. Then she disappears off the face of the earth.

'I've got it on screen,' Lucinda tells Graziane. 'The last sign of her is on a street near Guarulhos airport. Could there have been an accident?'

Graziane/Andreza says she has already called the hospitals and morgues across the entire state. And alerted her network of contacts. No one knows anything about Viviana.

'Have a look at where she went *before*,' says Graziane. 'Because she always lets me know when she goes to meet a client, tells me where she is, the client's name, and so on. It can't have been a job.'

Lucinda zooms out on the map until she can see the last place Viviana visited before all trace of her was lost. She recognises the address.

'You're right, Graziane, it definitely wasn't work.'

3

GRAZIANE

Andreza, or rather Graziane, hangs up and looks at the driver.

'Nearly there?'

'Almost,' he replies.

Cut up by lights at every corner, the traffic creeps slowly down a long São Paulo street. The number they're looking for is 3275, and they're only just into the two thousands, constantly checking the odd side of the road.

Graziane looks at her phone and reads.

I never really liked sleeping with photographers. 99% act like they're doing you a favour, or making a dangerous exception because you're not a woman, you know, you're a medium. A screen, an artistic material. Even when you're stark naked in front of them.

That's just it. I hate professionalism, hahaha.

But Jairo wasn't like that. He saw me as I really was – at least once the session was over. He had a very visible on/ off button, a light would go on inside and he'd go back to being a person again and, most importantly, see me as a person again. A desirable person. I won't talk about love, perhaps because it doesn't take much to satisfy me, simply knowing that someone desires my body for what it is and not as a platform for their 'art' or to gain another notch on the bedpost.

. . .

He liked to fuck her head-on. To be more specific, he liked it when her spine was slightly curved back, like the tip of a sleigh, and he could watch with each thrust how his cock rubbed against the soft part above the vulva. Such a clear reaction. It was the answer he wanted.

Vivi didn't moan much. That wasn't a bad thing, far from it: it challenged him to go even deeper. And nowadays there was a very disagreeable trend for women to do exaggerated moaning just to impress. Obviously it always ended up resembling a porno film, and obviously if he wanted a porno film he wouldn't be fucking her. Figure and ground.

. . .

'He withdrew from me and went to the toilet, leaving me there on my front. My monster's insides writhed languidly, wanting more. I moved one of my legs so that it could see the surroundings better, take some air.'

. . .

'I turned over and found a newly woven spiderweb. I went over to it and admired the strength of the fibres, hesitant

to touch it but knowing that I was only prolonging the
ritual. I offer up my fingers as a sacrifice and feel the
hungry creature devouring them until it's satisfied.'

That was one of the most striking passages in Vivi's diary –
and also a clue.

Back when Graziane first read it, she had given Viviana
her honest opinion: she adored the multiple erotic per-
spectives in her diary, but she was put off by knowing the
events and the characters whose real names she was using.
OK, it was only a matter of changing the names, but she
felt that would be difficult to publish at a time when there
was such a resurgence of narrow-mindedness. Graziane
had first gone on the game before she'd finished her
journalism degree. She had never worked as a journalist.
As well as helping her family she was trying to save money
to open up a business in her birth city in Paraná state –
preferably a bookshop and stationer's. The problem was
she couldn't balance her books and would spend everything she earned. Until Vivi came along.

Because she was living between Rio and São Paulo,
Viviana had offered Graziane her Rio apartment to use as
much as she wanted. That was the step Graziane needed
to take to consolidate her client base in Rio. It wasn't
pure altruism on Vivi's part: with Graziane on board she
could offer both blonde and brunette options to her
loyal gringos. Every city had its high and low seasons,
and sometimes each would go to their own corner to take
advantage of demand for a certain physical type. Viviana,
who spoke a little Japanese *(just a tiny bit,* she'd blush,

from watching too much anime), had optimised her revenue by improving her English and organising her finances. Graziane had savings now.

But what really sealed the deal was when Vivi went home with her and gave her that wonderful oral. Graziane often tried to repay her with her best technique, but she discovered that Vivi responded better to penetration. Her collection of erotic toys had never seen so much use, though her spine and her carpal tunnel sometimes felt the impact. Vivi orgasmed during work, Graziane did not, she was always on the brink. Vivi didn't mind being the active partner and Graziane kind of liked those semi-fixed roles, like an old-school lesbian couple. At work Vivi was always taken to be a fragile, soft-skinned little object, another semi-fixed role, when really she was such a versatile person. But when they worked as a pair no client ever objected to them taking time to eat each other out – even though they were being paid by the hour. It was the perfect crime.

Graziane knew it would be impossible to take Vivi to her home in Paraná and introduce her to the family as her partner. No way. Her parents and relatives, who asked her every Christmas holiday where her boyfriend was, wouldn't be able to take it in.

She also knew that the other girls didn't really like Viviana. Too successful. Aside from that, while on the one hand Viviana hid her work from her family (like all the other girls on the game), when she was with other colleagues she was in the habit of loudly philosophising about what she called 'our profession'. Graziane had hinted to Vivi that she shouldn't make such definitive statements about pride and identity to girls who nearly always concealed what they did, even to themselves. It was unbearable to hear, even for a prostitute.

Before Graziane, Viviana's head had been a whirlwind of ideas that almost never saw the light of day. Despite always being surrounded by people, she had no one to share her thoughts with. The diary, which was becoming a book, had also functioned as an escape valve. Graziane had been honoured to be chosen as her reader. And lover.

The two of them were symbiotically in love. Any time they were in the same city, no matter how exhausted from their respective appointments each was always ready to spoil the other with an orgasm, one woman totally focussed on the other. Or they'd just share a duvet, naked with the air conditioning on, watching a dumb movie, or just as often an arty one. Their feet touching, each of them reading a book on the sofa. They'd never had a serious talk about the relationship, but the bond was strong. Viviana's absence hurt Graziane. It wasn't the money, or the convenience, or the know-how; it was Viviana. She'd do anything to find her, wherever she was.

Now she had almost reached her destination.

'You know what, Tônio? Drive a little bit past the address. Slowly,' Graziane says.

As they drive past, Graziane sees, through a leafy flower bed, Jairo's car parked next to the studio. No one nearby other than a security guard.

'OK. You can pull over.'

Graziane pays Tônio and gets out of the car. She walks up to the enormous wooden door and positions herself below the security camera, so that only the top of her head can be seen. She presses the intercom button.

'Who is it?'

'It's Viviana, Jairo's expecting me.'

'One minute.'

Graziane contemplates the tip of her short-heeled boot and leans against the wall, a habit which Viviana has often criticised and tried to tame. It isn't the kind of thing a sophisticated woman does. It makes people think you've walked too far and need to sit down. You *never* need to sit down. But now Vivi isn't there and no one can say if she is anywhere. *What did they do with your body?* Graziane thinks about baths of acid.

She's roused by the loud click of the door opening. She looks up and sees Jairo Valdino, an incredibly tall white man with dark curly hair and almost no stubble. Graziane stares into his green eyes while he says:

'Grazi? You?'

He draws in his chin, surprised to see her there – not the good kind of surprise.

'Jairo. Can I talk to you?'

'I'm right in the middle of a session.'

'I know. That's why I said I was Viviana.'

'What is it?' he asks, adjusting his jeans around the belt. His hands stay on his waist, stabilising his body. It's not easy being a beanpole.

'Have you seen Vivi?'

'No, I haven't. Is that all? I've got work to do.'

'I know you're still seeing each other.'

'We're not still *seeing each other*.' Jairo sticks out his tongue.

'I've checked her location services. I know she was in your apartment.'

'Only to shoot some photos.'

'Photos of her naked by your window, with the city as backdrop. Ha!' Graziane throws her hair back and shakes her head. 'Look, I don't care, my relationship with her is far from exclusive. I just need to know if you've seen her this week.'

'I haven't.'

'Yesterday?'

'No. Why?'

'She's vanished.'

His expression undergoes a change that leaves Graziane feeling reluctantly satisfied. He's worried about Viviana. He hasn't done anything bad to her. Graziane realises that the security guard at the studio has positioned himself so that he can watch the scene unfold. The receptionist is surely doing the same. This much she expected.

'Vanished? Since when?'

'Not a trace of her since yesterday.'

'Have you spoken to the police?'

'Uh-huh, and her sister in Rio too.'

Graziane had thrown the bait of the century by talking about Vivi's visits to Jairo. She did in fact follow Vivi's footsteps a little more than necessary, but she knew nothing about what went on at these meetings. Nor did she care if they were fucking – she had a pussy and her openness to experiment going for her. He didn't. What she wanted was to strike fear into his heart by playing the jealous lover and seeing what came out. But, from the looks of it, there was nothing there.

'Do you think I did something to her?' Jairo asks, hand on heart, trying to look offended.

'No, Jairo…' She resists the urge to roll her eyes. 'But I think someone has. She wouldn't just disappear like that, without saying anything. Did she say anything the last time you saw each other, did she have any problems, was anyone making a scene? If she didn't say anything to me the only person she could have spoken to is you.'

Jairo thinks for a minute, then chooses to speak.

'Do you know who's in São Paulo? Just moved here?'

'Who?'

'Leo Faulhaber. From that site that Vivi…'

'I know.'

He hesitates again but ends up speaking:

'She mentioned it to me. Last week.'

There was a time when Viviana would spend the whole day posing. At twenty-one, as well as the jobs she was already doing, she was chosen to be one of the first models in a group of 'Brazilian faces' stock photos which an ex-journalist was compiling – *Gente*, People, it was called. It was hilarious. She loved telling that story.

In the showroom of a closed home goods store, Viviana was snapped with a good-quality, Chanel-cut wig, eating salad and laughing, cutting colourful vegetables on a chopping board, placing one in her mouth. Eyes closed.

Eyes open. Half-open. Beaming, wide-open eyes. Then in the background with her natural hair tied up in a Japanese-style bun, the same as her office colleague who is smiling out of focus, toasting the success of a black man in a suit positioned near the camera. Then cuddling up with an athletic, mixed-race model on the sofa, a cute couple pondering their next purchase together in front of a laptop, both laughing, then smiling, then serious, debating. Then it was time for bed to act out all the tiny variations needed for any material on The Sex Life of the Brazilian Couple. The insatiable Jairo had directed.

'Now sit on the bed and pull the covers up to your belly. Cross your arms. You're frustrated. Now hold this STOP sign… Turn it this way, that's it… a bit less… look the other way, sulking. Now still sulking but with a little smile. Now like you've just had it, you can't take it any more. That's it. Perfect. Now repeat all three, but this time he's frowning, like he's also pissed off. One. Two. Three. Excellent. Done.

'Now let's go out to the balcony. Hold this pregnancy test. Gaze into the distance. Smiling. Now anguished. Relax your face a bit.'

And Viviana did the thing where she massaged her face and made random expressions, a gimmick which Graziane knew from her modelling days and found hilarious.

Given the sheer novelty of images of people who actually looked like Brazilians, made for Brazilians, these photos spread far and wide and were still in circulation to this day, their high-resolution versions reacquired every time someone needed to use them to illustrate some material, book or advertising. The GENTE stock image bank was the only one to offer typically Brazilian and Latino faces; as well as being priced in reais and not in dollars, they showed up the other stock image faces as foreign. The royalties, meagre as they were, began landing in Jairo's account. Viviana received nothing beyond the fee for the shoot, but that work, which was assumed to be casual, a mere footnote, embarrassing even, ended up advancing her career. In parallel, she and the photographer began an affair which they took some time to acknowledge was a relationship, before ending as it had begun: as a friendship, against the odds.

At the time the two of them were an item – the sex was excellent, according to Vivi – Jairo was living away from São Paulo and Vivi only ever went there for sporadic jobs. Every date the couple went on ended up in a terrible cheap motel, which they travelled to and from in a taxi – neither of them had a car – the reception girl asking for their tax numbers and the two of them always declining to give them, as if that made the affair more illicit and exciting.

Though there was nothing stopping them, they didn't want to make any declarations of commitment, as Viviana's work was likely to get more challenging and Jairo was building his career in a nomadic fashion – carrying his home and his photographic equipment on his back, wearing a different shirt over the same trousers each day. Viviana began visiting São Paulo at every opportunity, with increasingly nebulous reasons, and began coughing up for hotels that were less grotty than the motels they were accustomed to. Jairo didn't want to admit it, but this was making him feel uncomfortable, and he was suspicious of where she was getting her money from.

One day Vivi announced that she'd got the keys to an aparthotel in the centre; after three years the two of them could finally meet in a respectable place whenever they were in São Paulo. Jairo couldn't contain himself and asked: 'Lucrative gig?', as he knew her rich grandfather had died and that Vivi's family no longer had the same income. She was about to add that she was even thinking about moving to São Paulo for good, to study his reaction, but instead she decided to reveal the origin of the cash. Jairo said he didn't want to be anyone's pimp. 'Oh, that's what you think?' she said, secretly not all that surprised at his reaction. Jairo thought about trying to make amends but preferred to stay silent. The steak they'd ordered on room service arrived; Viviana ate only the protein, paid the bill and left him there. Soon she'd leave the country too, in an attempt to soar higher. When she came back, years later, she was already involved with Graziane.

So it's not as if he hadn't accepted the separation, or that he regretted his behaviour. And to tell the truth, Graziane can't see Jairo hurting Vivi. But she is certain that if Viviana had a plan B it would involve him. And she suspects that Viviana might also have been his plan B. It's hard to tell. She had to sound it out.

Now it was time to visit someone who could quite easily have hurt her lover.

4

LUCINDA

Bookers, daddys, babys. *Translation: pimps, clients, hookers. Or if you prefer you can call them escorts, working girls, call girls. Things don't match the names they're given. Or rather: they perpetually gain new names to throw unwanted meddlers off the scent. I feel like an old lady talking this way, though I'm barely into my thirties. And the thirties are the new twenties anyway. So it's all good.*

The funny thing is that, in my case, I came upon this second profession precisely because I wasn't keen on this new usage, because I came across terms that did not match their true meanings.

Knowing how to pose is a kind of intelligence. Of course, that's not what they want you to think. They want you to think that a photographer is doing you a favour by choosing to immortalise you with his magnificent phallic lens, because you're just a doll – a mannequin, isn't that right?

But it's possible to use your own body as a framing suggestion. There's a special notion, some art in knowing how to be the passive member of the relationship. Knowing how to receive, like a host: my body, right here, offered up to the viewer and yet still unavailable. I have that ability,

*and it's worth a lot. And they don't know that I'm aware
of this value and that I know how to exploit it.*

And that's how we work.

• • •

You must want to hear about my first time.

*I was eating lunch alone in the food court of a São
Paulo mall, when a man dropped a folded slip of paper
with his number written on it onto my table. This man,
who was sitting on another table, had been staring at
me for some time, and without knowing why, I decided to
return his gaze. Actually, I do know why: because I felt like
testing my limits, seeing what would happen if I decided
to behave in a completely different way from how I felt;
to act, in short. The man was old and repulsive and yet
I looked back at him, to turn things up a notch. It was
like swallowing my own vomit, but I managed to hold his
gaze. When he got up, I thought he had simply left, but
after walking behind me and leaving his tray by the bin,
he stopped next to me and dropped the paper, with no
subtlety whatsoever, before walking straight off. I looked
at the scrap of paper as if it was a bit of pigeon shit that
had almost fallen into my beer.*

I picked it up, unfolded it and read.

*It had a very clear proposition on it, suggested payment
included, not just his mobile number. The guy must have
been waiting nearby. If I called, I could make two thousand
reais that afternoon. But would he really pay? Something
told me he would. He was the kind of old man who hides*

his money (he was eating fast food) and only spends it on titbits; this type of guy takes pleasure in splashing out on insignificant things and living in rented houses so that he has no assets to leave to his relatives, all of whom he considers to be 'a bunch of freeloaders'. In my family alone I have two uncles who fit this profile. Uncle Scrooges. And I was just a titbit, a snack before lunch. I understood this – and I knew I wanted to say yes. I just hadn't figured out why I wanted to say yes. That's why I took a while to accept.

I was eighteen years old and already quite experienced. I'd been with students, teachers, beach people, art people, street people, people who could get me work or had already got me work. Sometimes it was more effective not to give out, keep the promise just out of reach, bewitch the person. Sometimes I'd put out just to stop someone harassing me: it's easy to keep your boss at arm's length when you're fucking his boss. Sometimes I would have sex just to make someone I liked jealous, and that could be a strategic move as well as an act of despair. Sometimes I didn't even know if I was really choosing. Now: were these good reasons? That is, was there any lust in this story? Was I still feeling lust? Curiosity? Or were they becoming increasingly secondary motives? Was I moved only by the desire to gain money and power and control (and drugs)?

On this occasion there was no intermediary. I was sober. He wasn't in my circle. And the nature of the proposition was quite clear. The way I saw it, the old man was my opportunity for total control. To have my cake and eat it. He'd think I was the cake… while I ate him and his money.

The truth is that it was only my first time in the strict sense of the word. What I'd been doing up to then was barter: sex in exchange for power, attention, protection. As I surrounded myself with people involved in events, magazines, studios, there was always that background hum, that feeling that I had to offer something on the side, something extra, not just promises and suggestive looks. And sometimes, right, I'd actually fuck them. But I was always out of it. And sex was never the main thing. Never agreed upon, out in the open, written down. Now it was right in front of me, written down on that crumpled scrap of paper.

I said yes.

Thus, Vívian was born.

Or rather, incubated. Vívian only had a concrete existence on sporadic occasions until the agency, and myself, realised I was getting old. And until I realised that I had grown accustomed to certain material comforts that would begin to dry up. And that I would need more and more.

They say that women aren't good at separating the emotional from the sexual, that if they fuck someone they'll fall in love with them. That only women who are in love fuck, that they won't betray anyone they're in love with, etc. But when you work with sex you inhabit another reality: men are the ones who can't separate the emotional from the sexual. The young ones are even worse, the ones who've been educated by porn, who know little of life but think they know a lot. I avoid these types because they tend to be short on cash and always looking for variety, never going with the same girl twice, or if they do, for the wrong reason (that is, to take you away from that lifestyle).

The hard thing is getting the guy to objectify you properly. In other words, use you just for pleasure, play along with your acting, your false name, your acrylic nails. If he's the kind of guy who gets attached or feels disrespected, you'll suffer. You could get beaten up, have your contract broken. You could be obliged to smile while he tries to fuck you without a condom or in the wrong hole. You should refrain from talking back and telling him that with his calibre you probably won't feel much difference anyway. You'll shake him off by smiling or charging more later – that's all.

If you want to be an escort, you need to assume that they'll always try to short-change you and work on your defence without showing it. The sleight-of-hand learnt from porn, which involves tricking the woman, duping her, disorienting her, is part of the package for many clients. He can't get hard without it.

It's also important to avoid the dude who romanticises you and wants to turn you into his wife, the perfect lover. He wants you to belong only to him, and by choice. It's a very common fantasy for single men with dull sex lives. It's much safer to service guys who regularly go with escorts, the married guys in suits. Don't be tempted to diversify, it will only cause problems. (Like with Carlo or the dude in the restaurant.)

It was a diary, but knowingly written with publication in mind. Lucinda scrolls down Viviana's laptop screen and finds a more recent entry. The language, as she suspected, is now different:

All the things that society looks down on and doesn't want you to do – prostitution, BDSM, homosexuality, drugs – have something in common: society wants you to believe that if you ever so much as dabble then you'll never be free of it. There is no turning back. These people were absolutely overjoyed by HIV/AIDS, because it really was like that: no way back, it was just righteous, eternal, divine condemnation, you waste away and then you die, amen. Now there are cocktails, treatments, prophylactics, people can survive and stay healthy. They're creating a vaccine. Can it be that God has decided to grant us freedom again?

Hold your horses. We're this deep into the twenty-first century and the propaganda is as strong as ever. Smoked a joint? You'll die a crackhead. Fucked for cash? You'll never be a normal woman again. Taken it up the arse? You're a faggot and you always will be. Got off on a bit of spanking? You'll never enjoy vanilla sex again, etc. etc. But the sheer numbers of people who have experimented with such impure things and incorporated them into a normal lifestyle – bisexuals, weekend weed smokers, occasional escorts (me) – are there to tell you: it's all a myth. Don't take advice from people who have never enjoyed life, who have never ventured and never gained. If you want to try something, try it. It's quite possible – even likely – that you'll be able to obtain more forms of pleasure from life if you try several. In fact, it's normal for someone to incorporate a few of these things into their lives. No one can subsist the whole time on a single thing. Only in movies.

Her sister is writing a porno self-help book. God help us. It's going to sell millions.

'We're there, madam,' the driver says, turning to face her.

'Oh, sorry.' Lucinda closes the laptop, pays for the journey, puts the computer under her arm and gets out with her cabin-sized bag, wearing black trousers and a white blouse. She looks like an executive, or a desperate version of one. She looks around her, checking where to go and runs towards the airline check-in desk.

She keeps running as she considers that narrating sexy adventures has already made more than one Brazilian prostitute with a knack for personal branding rich. People have also made a fortune from the opposite phenomenon: look at all the things I did when I was possessed by demons, until Jesus saved me. Erotic self-help was a less well-mined source. Did Viviana really have the courage to publish that? Under her own name? Perhaps she did, for the money, of which there would doubtless be a considerable amount.

Yes, but she wasn't showing any remorse. She didn't seem remotely contrite for having chosen the easy life without really needing to, without a starving child or a tragic story of poverty and abuse. Sexy, intelligent and in control of her own life: was Brazil ready to receive this slap in the face?

Vívian was her hooker name. *Vívian.* The cheek of Viviana: flirt with danger by removing a single letter from your name and use what remained as a nom de guerre, of all the options she had at her disposal. But it was good enough, Lucinda had to admit. Viviana was a rich person's name, an exclusive name, which she'd never encountered among people she knew; their mother had chosen it after carefully studying all the possible options and spellings in baby name books, wracking her brains for months for that unexpected second girl. And she had settled upon Viviana for the new baby. Not Vívian or Viviane, as was common. A Europeanised name. By removing one letter a nice pseudonym had emerged, with a different aspect. It became a hooker's name. The name of the hooker from *Pretty Woman*. It was so Vivi: hiding in plain sight.

Her name, Lucinda, suggested petticoats and chivalric romances. It was her Indigenous Great-grandmother's Christian name, Cássia's way of honouring her. She hardly ever used that name any more. Her mother and sister called her Lucy, which was shorter and more affectionate and intimate. In her teenage years, her embarrassment at her full name made her start introducing herself as Cindy, which at the time she found foreign and sophisticated but in retrospect was just hard to make out over the din of a nightclub. After puberty nothing left her more furious that when people discovered her real name and called her by it. She had made a fake ID with the name Lucy on it, but sometimes Lucinda was revealed during the school register or when someone was sufficiently switched on to realise that if you joined together the two names, Lucy + Cindy, you got Lucinda. Nowadays she liked her Christian name: she felt it gave her an air of ancient wealth, nobility even.

But then Cássia had a second daughter and had to be… creative. So many illustrious grandfathers waiting to be paid tribute to, and another girl had come along. Then that was it.

Lucinda checks her mobile. The clock reads 2:58 p.m. She's put up the stupid post with the news of her sister's disappearance and a photo of her. People have reached out, shared, offered their sympathies, but no one's given any information. Her mother still hasn't seen or heard her messages. She must be really enjoying herself on a boat trip or something, but eventually she'll get back to the hotel and discover what's happening.

Sitting in the airport departures lounge, Lucinda does a search for her own name in one of the folders on Viviana's laptop. It appears in just one file, cuts.docx.

It's doubly exhausting to try and live peacefully with someone who is competing with you. In fact it would be less effort just to openly compete than to continually avoid doing so, as I've been doing with my older sister Lucinda for as long as I can remember. Well, since before we were teenagers anyway.

'Of course you don't want to compete: you don't need to! It's *hors concours*, you'd win too easily, wouldn't you? It wouldn't be good for Miss Superior's image to be competing against such a weak opponent. Now you've vanished, you might be dead. And me, I've got to read this shit,' thinks Lucinda before she continues reading.

My sister is a classic example of the sins of the 90s. Competitive. Compulsive. Bulimic. Our mother took us to a psychologist at the same time, but it was obvious who needed the treatment most.

'Yeah, you!' Lucinda thinks.

She thought she was the queen of the hard-done-by, dividing women into slags/sluts/tarts and her, the saint. So superior.

'Oh, get fucked!' Lucinda says out loud, attracting the curious gaze of her neighbour on the bench and closing the file by angrily clicking directly on the x. How could she write that *with a view to publish*? OK, it was in a file called 'cuts' – she had decided not to publish it. But still, the sheer bile!

Even so, Lucinda feels she should be more forgiving. Viviana's missing, a hot plate of a thought she doesn't want to hold in her hands. And she knows Vivi's history all too well.

There had been diagnoses – dysthymia, schizoid personality disorder and even Asperger's, when Vivi was very young and almost never spoke, only read. (For Lucinda it was anxiety, panic, bulimia. The anxiety was real, a perennial truth; the panic would go and – at times – return; the bulimia was today a distant, sickening nightmare.) Lucinda remembers having been impressed and a little jealous when her six-year-old sister had received a warning from school for having 'invaded' the 'teenage section' of the library and read books that were not 'appropriate for her stage of psychosocial development'. Lucinda knew that the library did not have sections separated by age and that every pupil was picking up and reading books with potentially racy content. Later Lucinda understood that the school had given Vivi the warning simply because it didn't know what to do with her, as she didn't like socialising and sometimes got into fights, and so they had come up with an excuse for Cássia to take command of the problem and take her daughter to a child psychologist.

Little by little Viviana learnt to pass as normal among her group, to resemble just another one of her little white friends. At least as far as possible. The act was incorporated into her way of being. Perhaps acting was her ideal job, her vocation. And it was clear that her distant manner precluded any serious interrogation. It was almost impossible to strike up a conversation with her and obtain something in exchange, however much you really knew her. Even if the person felt it was worth persisting, they'd give up before they got to the important part, defeated by Vivi's terseness, her insurmountable beauty and her well-rehearsed charisma. Lucinda had witnessed this innumerable times; she had watched her sister perfect it over the course of her adolescence. Nowadays that training must have made it easier to ignore the married men's wedding rings. That is, if she ever felt remorse, and assuming they kept the ring on.

But Lucinda knows her sister from before, long before. And she doesn't judge her – or rather, she does, but she also has sufficient evidence to absolve her. Even when she was a successful model, Viviana had always maintained a secret world in which she could still be a child and – perhaps most importantly – cultivate imaginative hobbies. First it was a passion for superheroes, especially female ones. At twelve she was always frequenting any news-stands that sold imported comics. Then she started downloading them all online. She never mentioned this to her classmates. If a friend ever came over to the house Viviana would say that the books and comics they saw belonged to her older sister, and Lucinda would let it go, thinking it an understanding and selfless gesture. Later Vivi went through a phase of watching fan-subtitled anime and collecting manga, even taking private lessons in Japanese with a professor from Niterói. With time, her tastes became more alternative and refined: classic literature, arthouse cinema, vinyl LPs. At the same time she kept up the model lifestyle, the image of a frivolous girl. It's not a facade: both Vivis are real. Her sister has always gone to great efforts to keep everything in different compartments, although a lack of internal communication makes her slow to reveal her own feelings to herself. Perhaps that's why she chooses to write: putting it on paper or on the screen is a way of suppressing that deficiency. Anyway, Lucinda is no psychologist, nor is she a detective, and yet here she is.

She went over to her sister's apartment with the aim of discovering her whereabouts, looked up her most recent transactions and kickstarted the process of collective searching and worrying, nudging the social networks with her first post: 'My sister went to São Paulo and hasn't made contact since yesterday. Worried! Has anyone been in touch with her?'

And she also discovered *that*.

When she made the post she knew people wouldn't sympathise as much if that side of Viviana's life was revealed. Not a bit. Viviana is lucky it's her sister doing the investigating.

She can sit on that bomb and stop it from exploding. She knows how to approach it with equal amounts of emotion and detachment, because both will be necessary.

Let's recap. A client might be to blame for Viviana's disappearance. It might be a jealous colleague or a vengeful pimp. It might have to do with drugs. But it might also be nothing of the sort; perhaps it isn't even a genuine disappearance.

Lucinda would be suspicious of any police investigation where they knew her sister was a hooker. And she knows it would be futile to explain Viviana's whole story to any professional investigator and how she has other areas in her life that are just as important. That she has gained enemies in every realm, people who hate her and might want to hurt her, because she is beautiful, because she shines too bright, because she is a mixed-race woman who doesn't bow her head in submission. Lucinda carries this intimacy like a trump card, trying to convince herself of the right thing to do.

She's worried about the moment her mother finally gets a connection, discovers her messages and calls. Cássia has been trying to recover from her exhaustion and Lucinda is about to burst onto the scene and tell her that her daughter is still missing; she can hardly use the same call to reveal Viviana's second profession. Lucinda is scared of feeling cornered and blurting something out. She's also scared of telling her about Graziane. The uncertainty is a total nightmare.

15:02. The flight to São Paulo will leave from one of those low gates, via a bus, and she shuffles around in her chair, finding new reasons to be on edge. She'd stressed to the airline receptionist that she needed to get to Guarulhos quick and they'd gone and put her on this flight? She should have blurted out something like 'It's a matter of life or death!!!', preferably in tears. She'd found it difficult to get across what she actually felt. At the same time, she also felt she had some right to privacy, that it was possible to resolve things without creating a scandal. Yeah, right. Now wasn't the time for keeping up appearances. Perhaps she hadn't seemed desperate enough. Or perhaps – she thinks as she looks at the attendant – she hadn't appeared rich enough. Card on desk, 'I'll pay whatever it costs.'

Besides, Lucinda doesn't have much faith in the police. Yes, she had followed that officer's recommendation that she send them her sister's photo via WhatsApp, and she had been sent the missing person poster for Viviana, but that was all they seemed to be doing. Perhaps it would be better to hire a private detective. But the one thing her mother, speaking as a lawyer, always said about PIs was that the overwhelming majority of them resolved nothing – that is, when they weren't professional black-mailers or using the information they obtained to carry out kidnappings or a scam. Lucinda wouldn't know which names were trustworthy and wouldn't risk anything on a matter of such importance. Until Cássia makes contact, Lucinda is the most suitable person to investigate. Or the least unsuitable. Along with Graziane, who has just written to her about the outcome of the meeting she had with Viviana's ex: he doesn't seem to be guilty. Now Graziane is going after the golden boy who had harmed

Vivi's career some time ago. She says she knows exactly how to deal with him.

Lucinda remembers how painful and unpleasant that incident was. She had watched everything from up close; it wasn't impossible that this was the guilty party. She decides to tell Graziane some information about the people involved in that affair. That's something she can do to help.

Meanwhile, she boards for Guarulhos, headed for the last location recorded on Viviana's mobile. It's easier for her to fly there than for Graziane to drive out from central São Paulo. Apart from anything else, she wanted to check the place out herself. The eight-digit access code for Vivi's bank account, which could not be the account holder's phone number, was kept in a file in her My Documents folder. It was their mother's number with the first digit missing. Lucinda could have thought of this in the three attempts she had been given if she hadn't been in the worst state possible for inferring things. Three cheers for the incautious user who writes their password down in a notebook – it would come in handy in a situation such as this.

What Lucinda had found there wasn't debt, as she was expecting, but sufficient funds to put down a deposit on an apartment. Clearly her sister is prostituting herself with an economic goal. And she sure is focussed...

However, in her statements from the last six months, which was as far back as the bank let you see, there are substantial transfers made to one account. Every month Viviana had made at least one transfer, sometimes more.

They definitely weren't debts. Some kind of blackmail, maybe?

Combining this knowledge with the place where the last credit card transactions were recorded and the geo-location shown by her sister's phone, indicating an address in Guarulhos, Lucinda knows exactly who to look for.

5

GRAZIANE

Graziane reaches the Vila Mariana address at around four thirty in the afternoon, after having visited the website of Leonardo Faulhaber's newly opened co-working space in São Paulo. It's a two-storey house with a white and terracotta facade, recently refurbished from the looks of it, with an iron gate and a small garden of pots and flower beds. The rustic frontage is decorated with an acrylic sign held in place by aluminium spacers: Master Plan – Creative Space. Graziane pulls the latch, pushes open the gate and enters. She tries to peep through the clear part of the frosted-glass panel of the front door, but as she can't make out anything inside she pushes open that door too.

There's no one in the room. She sees coloured cushions tossed into a corner and a long worktop with just a computer on it, turned off. At the back, a pile of half-undressed colourful surfboards can be glimpsed, peeping out from their black covers, not used recently from the looks of it, along with part of a wetsuit. The smell of sweat tempered by disinfectant seems to dominate the air – or maybe that's just her impression. Is Leo even here?

She thinks of calling out for him but changes her mind. If Leo hears a woman's voice she might give away the element of surprise. Treading softly, Graziane continues towards what looks like a sink and kitchenette.

On the website, Leonardo announced that anyone hiring a co-working space would have the right to a coaching session with the comedian Leo Faulhaber, one of the creators of *Wild Pumpkin*. At the foot of the paragraph, he added: 'Limited availability owing to other commitments.'

Graziane detects a soft sound on the floor above as she walks past the staircase. She decides to go up, making some noise this time. As she ascends the final steps, she spots Leo's blond mane, which, at least from behind, hasn't receded all that much for a man well into his thirties; Leo's neck decorated by a pair of those big branded headphones which cover only part of the ear without fully blocking out noise; Leo's back in a yellow T-shirt; Leo's butt in grey cargo shorts; and, last of all, Leo's calves – one of them shaved, tattooed and wrapped in clingfilm. Standing still behind him at the top of the stairs, Graziane smiles. She reaches forward and gently squeezes his shoulder.

Leo jumps, pulls off his headphones and turns to face her.

'That's why you didn't answer…' Graziane says. 'Heey, Leo.'

'Hey.' He doesn't know her, but thinks that he should, and looks intrigued. 'Sorry, you are…?'

Graziane lets a straight, controlled smile form on her face and extends her hand.

'You don't know me. Graziane Novicki. Pleased to meet you.'

His eyes twinkle as they try not to look her body up and down, but nevertheless slide down towards her low, not too deep neckline.

'Likewise, Graziane. Leo.' He shakes her hand and scratches his head with the other, feigning embarrassment. 'Sorry about that. I was here, writing a script... deep in concentration.'

He takes on the part of the ultra-friendly host.

'So, then. Are you interested in the space?' he asks, turning the screen off and starting to walk around. 'Wait a moment, I'll make some coffee, take a seat.'

Leonardo heads for the kitchenette while Graziane sits on a nearby sofa. Leo halts in front of a white Formica counter, chooses one of the coffees from the shelf above it and empties some into the grinder.

'Am I limping a lot? I got inked today. Three-hour session...' he says, showing a pained smile.

It looks as if he's in no hurry to find out why she's there. Graziane decides to play along to see how far he'll go.

'Oh right? Who with?'

'Jorgina Terêncio. Know her?'

'No.'

'A friend's girlfriend. She's really good.'

He sticks out his leg so she can see as he makes the coffee. Graziane inspects the tattoo. It's a mandala on his calf. He hasn't asked for any special cross-hatching or some other more refined technique. Graziane nods and says, with a light touch of sarcasm:

'She did a great job.'

Leo places a cup of coffee on the table in front of her and Graziane turns down his offer of sugar, which earns her praise. He respects anyone who can appreciate an unadulterated coffee. Graziane buys some time, lets him talk about the space, the rental charges per day, week and month. When he mentions the coaching, she decides to get to the point. She slaps her thigh softly.

'To be honest, I came here for a different reason,' she says in her velvety tone. She pauses, holding back her revelation. 'The truth is I'm more interested in the coaching than the space. I couldn't believe it when I found out you were in São Paulo.' In a slow, expansive movement she places her hands on her chest, giving him the perfect excuse to look at her breasts again. 'I'm *Wild Pumpkin*'s biggest fan. I don't want to say "I was" because I know you guys will be back some day.'

Leo's mouth starts to open into a smile, covering his teeth with his lips. He's amused. Mildly flattered.

'Ah, come off it, Graziane.'

'Call me Grazi!' She goes to town on the sharp, enthusiastic inflections, as if everything ended in an exclamation mark. 'I read it more than anyone else in my town. I *always* left a comment. You guys moderated it yourselves, didn't you? Remember Grazi51? No? Damn, it ended so suddenly. And the way it played out, so... low.'

'Yeah, that was...' His face shows signs of nostalgia, but barely any resentment.

'And that woman accusing you of *racism*...? She just wanted money, right? Or at least attention, because it's not like she had any talent. I bet she disappeared.'

Which indeed she has, Graziane thinks, watching the man's expression, which takes on a false air of benevolence.

'Look, Grazi, I don't hold grudges, you know? It's bad for the soul. It's all good from where I am. We went to the same school, you know? If I met her on the street today I'd just say hi and keep walking. That did actually happen when we lived near each other in Rio. People even called Viviana the "Yoko Ono of Brazilian comedy". So over the top. Between the two of us, *Pumpkin* had already done everything it could. Internet humour has changed a lot since 2002. Now it's all about memes, it's more politically correct. It evolved. And we weren't able to keep up.'

'Ah, don't say that!' she protests.

'It's true, I've no problem saying it. It's always best to stop when you're ahead. Why keep going? Just to turn into a dinosaur? Each of us went down our own path and it was better that way. Chico kept the site up just to stop some opportunist from claiming the domain name. He became a programmer. And now I'm scripting a series for a streaming service...'

Graziane sees that, despite his cordial manner, he's telling the truth. Bearing a grudge against Vivi and attempting to sully her image doesn't fit with the vision he has of himself and is trying to project here: a nice guy, funny, sensitive but not to the point of being a bore. Leonardo would never harshly criticise a friend in public; from another angle, openly going after Vivi would not be in good taste, however much she had harmed him by exposing his hypocrisy and his partner's racism. He had little to lose, since falling out of favour with the public was highly improbable, not to mention bankruptcy. Even in the worst-case scenario, that surfer–screenwriter, son of an ambassador and real estate don in the South Zone of Rio de Janeiro, would never find himself short of two pennies to rub together. In any case, Graziane isn't all that concerned about him or Chico.

'What about Walter? What's he done since?' she asked.

'I don't know, thank God.' Leo sips his coffee. 'We stopped speaking after all that stuff.'

'Serious?'

'Yeah. At that point he was beginning to spend a lot of time with those forum types, the ones who call women… nasty things,' he adds, censoring himself. 'Walter had given me carte blanche to look after the channel, but when he found out I'd hired an actress, a *woman*, and saw her face… he lost it. He showed up at the studio out of the blue, wanting to mark his territory and fill my ears with shit.'

'So he's the one who said all that shit about her?'

'He sure was! All of it! He said she looked like a domestic, he went on and on. The truth is he wasn't right in the head even back then. He never was. Around that time he started getting too involved in drugs and he fell in with the wrong crowd. He wanted to be a guru to the people on the forums, and he began half using *Pumpkin* as a platform to bring together his narrow-minded followers. There was nothing humorous about it any more. Just political. I didn't like it. He fought back. That was precisely when the stuff with Viviana happened.'

'What a mess. And where's he now, what's he doing?'

'He's… in Europe, I think.' Leonardo takes his mobile from his back trouser pocket and checks. 'Yep, in Amsterdam. I don't follow his Instagram any more, but it's easy to remember: walter.xxx.'

'Does he ever come back?'

'No, he's there illegally. Also, a guy like him? He won't come back. Over there he's got weed, hookers…'

Graziane looks down at her own neatly done nails. *Weed* and *hookers* reverberate in her head. She needs to grab her phone as soon as she can to find out everything about this Walter, now that she knows where he hides on the internet. She knows it can't have been him – but maybe one of his lapdogs in Brazil? Weirded out by her silence, Leonardo asks her:

'What is it?'

'It's nothing, I've just been thinking.' Graziane moves up to accommodate Leo, who has suddenly come over to sit on her side of the sofa. 'About putting myself forward as a writer or actress for *Pumpkin* if you guys decided to make a comeback. But from the looks of it there's no chance, right?'

Leo looks at Graziane, delighted, and stretches his lips out over his teeth in a gummy grin of understanding. He breathes in, seemingly wanting to take in her feminine scent, while trying to keep looking into her light-coloured eyes with an awed, voracious expression.

'No chance for the time being,' he says finally, slowly, edging closer to her. 'Who knows though, maybe one day, another project…'

With each word, he moves a few millimetres closer.

But Graziane moves away. She grabs her bag calmly and confidently and gets ready to stand up.

'Going already? Why not leave a card so we can arrange the coaching for another time?' he says, straightening up.

Graziane laughs.

'I didn't think people gave cards any more. You want my number?'

'Definitely.'

She grabs some paper and a pen from her bag and writes it down.

'Thanks,' he says. 'I'll see you downstairs.'

Leo follows her downstairs; the two of them cross the living room-cum-lobby, and he opens the door for her. Graziane thanks him for the coffee and kisses him goodbye on the cheek before slipping away through the threshold. For a moment he stands there watching her through the transparent part of the frosted glass. What just happened? What did that woman really want from him? Why did she move off when they were so close together on the sofa? Did she take it badly? Graziane pushes the gate and walks onto the street without looking back. It seems he had nothing to offer her.

Leonardo turns back, looks at the surfboards and longs for the sea.

In the taxi, Graziane sends Lucinda a voice note.

'So. It wasn't them. Not Leo or Walter. Leo doesn't give a damn about her. Walter's still an asshole, but he's living in Amsterdam and can't get back to Brazil, because he's there illegally.'

Her words come out in a descending tone; she's disappointed after going down another cul-de-sac.

'Are you at Guarulhos yet? Let me know when you get there, OK? I think I'll swing by Vivi's place, see if I can find anything.'

She gives a summary of the conversation with Leonardo and sends Lucinda Walter's Instagram so she can check it.

Ten minutes later, Lucinda lands in Guarulhos, reconnects and listens to Graziane's message. She looks at the photos of Walter on Instagram. She reaches the same conclusion as Graziane.

Leonardo Faulhaber had been a schoolmate of Viviana and Lucinda's from an early age. He was the same age as Lucinda and was in the same class as her for a long time until he had to repeat a year. At school he was famous as the kid who'd printed Goatse out as a poster and taken it into the classroom; the kid who'd won a competition to find a name for a fancy-dress party by coming up with 'The Sweaty Ball' (vetoed by the head teacher); and the co-founder of the fanzine *Hare-Brained Scheme* in their second year, with Chico Matsushita and Walter Bonelli. The zine-making trio then went to the same media school as Lucinda, and once the hazing and the undergrad drinking sessions were over they resurrected the zine as a website, taking the opportunity to change the name: it would now be called *Wild Pumpkin*. To start with, the site didn't have much of an identity: it published long articles that tore into celebrities, reviewed drugs and philosophised about different sexual practices; it made opportunistic visual jokes about the gaffe *du jour* or the big film coming out – which would then become known as a meme, and not in the sense they had been taught in Theory 101. Leonardo then established himself as the one who sorted out sponsorships, partnerships and freebies. A little later, two new things happened: the site stopped being able to cope with the huge number of views, and the trio received their first 'love letter' from a justice official, sent on behalf of a young *sertanejo* singer whom *Wild Pumpkin* had forced out of the closet. The new site was hosted on a Croatian server to discourage court cases, took on the form of a blog and began putting a watermark on its content to stop uncredited sharing. In the middle of university, Leonardo, Chico and Walter began delivering *Jackass*-style challenges to internauts, until they realised they could no longer fund all these controversies and court cases: they preferred to earn money in a simpler way. Then the content took on a more innocuous tone, at least from a legal point of view. The last time Lucinda remembered hearing about them was when they were taken over by a big web company. That was until 2014.

That year Viviana, only recently back in Brazil, had commented excitedly to Lucinda: 'Remember Leo Faulhaber, from school? He's opening a video channel for his site. He said he wants to change the way they operate but keep the same spirit, and he thought of me. The first female member of *Wild Pumpkin*, what an honour,' Vivi had said, sarcastically. 'But what matters is it will be my debut as a comedy actress. It's perfect because, if it's the way I think it is, you need to be serious for the joke to work, you know? It's the first job I've got where I'm *not* meant to smile.'

Later on, Leo had admitted to Viviana that he felt he was getting old, losing touch with what was popular in the world of comedy. One day, after a long morning surfing, having risen at dawn due to insomnia, Leo had concluded that if their strongest competition was adolescent vloggers, the way to counter them was to produce videos, which if done right could even lead to future TV contracts. So he made arrangements and started a *Wild Pumpkin* YouTube channel, with comedy sketches scripted by him and Chico. But something was missing, until Leo remembered Viviana.

At the time, Lucinda had thought: why Vivi? Sure, there was that whole cool attitude which Leo and his bros always tried to give off and which Viviana was the epitome of. This persona of hers was an act, but they didn't need to know; besides, even if they did know they wouldn't mind. There was also the awful trope of hot women playing highly sexualised parts in Brazilian comedy sketches. Thinking about it, being mixed race Viviana would take on the role of an 'alternative' sex symbol, fitting to the new era. Lucinda didn't want to mention it to her sister, but she kept exploring this thought: Viviana's physical appearance would also be enough to silence those who had accused *Pumpkin* of machismo, racism and homophobia, which drove away some internauts and sponsors.

The audio that went viral a few weeks later on social media, having been captured in the editing suite on a phone discreetly planted there by Vivi, contained choice lines such as 'It's a shame she looks like a domestic' and 'Lovely hair, you could almost believe it belongs to her'. They all came from Walter, but nevertheless Viviana condemned the 'complicit silence' from Leo, who in response had stated that this was unfair and accused Viviana of having made a 'selective edit' of the conversation. Neither the site nor the channel survived this, and the same went for Leo and Walter's friendship.

What really got Lucinda's goat at the time was Leo saying that Walter's behaviour had been an unfortunate coincidence, and not the result of a nasty trajectory going all the way back to when the snake first emerged from the egg, from that first dumb zine at that moronic school. Leo said that Walter had 'gone mad', the poor thing – and not simply turbocharged the racist misogyny that had always been there – and that he, Leo, had neither tried to mop up the dirt or stayed silent – contrary to what the audio recorded by Viviana showed – but *had been arguing with his friend since way before all this stuff came out*, and that the audio shared by Viviana had simply been an isolated incident in a day in the life of that knight errant of Brazilian comedy. Even if the audio hadn't surfaced, Leo had guaranteed, he was still intending to close the site and cut ties with Walter. This version, in which the mighty, heroic Leo came to the fore, was the one he told himself. At the same time it painted him as a mere victim of circumstances, destiny's plaything. Lucinda could see he was nothing more than a pathetic chancer, used to employing any kind of deception that would keep the flame of his own self-love alight.

Ultimately, though, at the very bottom of the pot of her misery, Lucinda had discovered her own morsel of blame in that episode. She had considered it opportunistic of her sister to share the audio. She was sceptical as to whether Vivi was truly shocked; she thought she simply wanted self-promotion. Of course, she offered her sister unconditional public backing, sharing the audio on social media and staunchly defending her, even fighting with strangers online – because, at the end of the day, she was her sister. But deep down, she betrayed Vivi in her thoughts, and now she feels like a piece of shit, because Viviana was right. Now she can clearly see what her sister had seen.

6

LUCINDA

Aeroplanes feel small to Lucinda. When possible she buys seats offering extra space, but even then she feels hemmed in. She sticks out a leg diagonally before drawing it in. Then she does the same with the other one. This movement helps stop her legs from seizing up. A tip she's learnt from fat friends is to always wear a skirt on plane journeys. Lucinda doesn't like skirts so she's wearing leggings.

Knickers tend to get stuck in the gap between her buttocks when she walks, sits or gets up. It's even worse on planes. She has to shove her hand down the back of her leggings and yank them from one side to another. Before initiating this procedure, Lucinda checks to make sure her neighbour is distracted. There's no one sitting between them and the man in the aisle seat is gazing gleefully at an air hostess's pert bum as she packs some bags into the overhead locker. Lucinda attends to her own behind and settles into the seat.

At thirty-five, Lucinda no longer doubts she is a sensual woman – she knows this and sometimes she thinks everyone knows, that they've always known, only they've never admitted it. Some guys sought her out when they were in town or when they saw her alone at a party, for example. They would head straight for her. But few wanted to go further and have the fattie who was taller than them as a girlfriend.

She'd been having casual sex way before apps for that purpose existed, but more recently she'd also been exploring the world of BDSM, signing up to sites aimed at that crowd. She had met people who liked to be tied up or tie people up, who were into being spanked or spanking (or burning and nipple twisting). Lucinda doesn't really know what she likes – or, as she puts it on her profile, she doesn't know yet, but she is prepared to find out. Her most frequent partner in such experiences is Nelson, who likes some of these things and seems to like her too, even if she is scared, deep down, that she is simply satisfying his fetish for strong, fat Amazons. It's all so new and strange, but what to do? She's beginning to admit to herself that she enjoys this or that practice. And him. Nelson is a little younger than her, and she considers him a promising catch, but she still doesn't want to call him her boyfriend. This is partly because her last serious relationship was with a man from a different generation, ten years older, kind of past his prime and horribly obsessed with being a macho Latin guy. He would always cheat on women, or at least attempt to, and only felt normal when acting that way. He wouldn't allow any questioning regarding his finances and would never even consider splitting domestic chores. He would retaliate in malicious and subtle ways if she got tipsy or really went for it on the dance floor at a party or chose to wear a short dress or a bold lipstick. He would humiliate Lucinda as a joke whenever he could, to show her who wore the trousers in the relationship, and play dumb when confronted. Lucinda grew tired of it. She had also realised that all her uncles and older cousins were, in one form or another, skilled readers from the same hymn sheet.

At least guys who were a little younger had some potential to be good partners. But that wasn't the case with the ones who were much younger; they had been largely educated by widespread and unrestricted porn and, having swallowed its narratives, were beginning to casually attack woman as a way of exercising power, calling them whores, fat, feminazis – in short, they'd sampled the misogynist poison being offered up on the chans and begun to rot from the inside (so young!). What was different about the decent men from the generation in between, what good influence had they been graced by? Lucinda was tempted to think that it could have been their exposure to girl power in the 1990s, not just the diluted Spice Girls version. And their difficulty in accessing porn because of their lack of a decent internet connection and credit card. It's possible that they had actually desired real, flesh-and-bone girls, beaten off while thinking about them and ejaculated. And that meant that this group of men were slightly more likely to see women as individuals. Lucinda wasn't sure if her theory was correct, but the guys she knew who were like that fit the age profile perfectly.

Lucinda's memories of that era were that being a woman 'with a personality' had meant something. No one wanted to be thought of as 'shallow'. Beauty was still almost everything, but it wasn't enough just to be beautiful. You needed to know something about the person behind that image to admire her – even if it was a poorly constructed sham. Minor variations on the archetypal virtuous warrior woman were served up for consumption in video games, music, all over, crying out to be imitated. But in real life it was unsightly to be complex, to reveal machismo for what it was, to fight for space. It was threatening. That's why Viviana went to such effort to conceal her cultural tastes, even after being a nerd became acceptable in the noughties.

It occurs to Lucinda that, even among the middle generation, the imprint of the Special Girl still had to be got rid of. The ideal of the selfless girl with a secret life of platonic hobbies, who hides them out of a kind of modesty, who knows she doesn't need make-up or skimpy clothes to draw attention to her perfect body and is laying on the charm just for *you*, average man. Then, just like that, she becomes *your* secret treasure, without you having done any work whatsoever. This bionic virgin nerd also appeared in some films. This false idol had to be torn to pieces or there'd be no end to it. Maybe that's what her sister was so hell-bent on doing.

By reading and integrating all this new info on her missing sister into the stories about her she knew first-hand, Lucinda felt closer both to Vivi and to a breakthrough about the case. It was also a way to keep her mind off the worse possibilities; the anxiety of examining them too closely would render her brain useless. She couldn't afford that.

The plane starts to taxi and Lucinda fidgets in her chair, looking urgently for something in the bag at her feet. She's transferred Vivi's diary/book to her e-reader and started reading it as a way of dealing with the ordeal of take-off.

How to define the character who gets me places in life: the party girl?

It's like that Sia song, the one that begins 'Party girls don't get hurt'. But not the depressing bit, the positive bit. Being that person who is the life of the party, who is the party. She's even the soundtrack to the party.

There she is, somewhere between Holly Golightly and Nomi Malone. She's well travelled, she's cool, never on a downer. She loves to have fun. The party girl entertains herself by drinking, dancing and fucking. And once she's done one or more of these things she'll open her mouth and sing, full-on a cappella, or grab the nearest instrument (if there is one) and improvise. Almost like a geisha and her shamisen.

Unlike most escorts, the party girl brings nothing to the party. No weight or responsibilities. She's let loose. Nothing to hold her down. In order to achieve this she has to have a trustworthy sidekick, carrying a bigger bag with condoms and other bits and pieces.

You're so good at your job – being the life of the party – that no one feels they have the right to deprive the party of you. You're the one who maintains the party's uninhibited, celebratory atmosphere, who gives the spark to that sense that everything is permitted, though it isn't really. Taking you off the stage would ruin everything. That's why you never need to say no twice (not 'no': 'in a minute', like a mother putting off a snack).

At any house party there's a specific moment, once enough guests have arrived, when things heat up. That's when the party girl takes the initiative: she knows it's time to stop cheerleading and to get into the game, pretending to be crazier than she actually is. Calling her friend to get up onto the table (if it's made of wood) and dance with her. Balancing on her heels and wearing only knickers while she checks to see if her friend is still at the other end of the table (or else it'll tip over). A very well-concealed calculation.

Not everyone knows how to behave at these events. Sometimes there are jealous people or people who aren't in the mood. The party girl may need to camouflage those people's reactions so that they look more into it than they really are. Or create a distraction so no one realises they've gone out to the balcony to smoke as they contemplate the ocean, all misty-eyed.

And there's nearly always sea nearby. When I think about this kind of party I see myself in Fortaleza, in Recife or with gringos in Rio. Or in Brasília, where the ocean is formed of plains and parched clouds. Far more frequent are the aborted plans or the improvised three-somes that occur in the heat of a work trip, at the hotel porter's suggestion. But even more frequent than that are the one-on-one encounters, just me and the client, after a ritual attempt at seduction in a civilised or even not so civilised setting. It's easier to prove to yourself you're

better than everyone else in a hotel room alone with a
girl you don't know. There will be no one to contradict
whatever version of the evening you decide to tell your
friends. Still, I like talking about these parties, where my
work doesn't just involve sex, but social manipulation,
behaviour coordination, interpreting patterns. Of course,
it's not such a big leap from this to basically being a
madame, or at least my own agent.

For Lucinda, the book seems a little undercooked: fragments without much to connect them together. Even so,
she likes what she reads.

I'm too old to be easily duped now and yet my appearance
still invites people to try to trick me, something that will
involve a lot of hard work for nothing. You'll think it's worth
the effort to try; I won't react badly to your advances even
though I should. You'll think it's fine to squeeze my neck
'just a little', despite what we'd agreed. You'll tell me you
prefer to pay after the hook-up and not before; you'll try
to shove it in the other hole while we're fucking; you'll tell
me you're faithful to your wife and would it be OK to do
it without a condom? A jumbo-size non sequitur as I look
into the gullible sucker's face. Finally, in my sweetest voice,
I say: Sorry, stud, it's not happening. No can do… sorry.

Lucinda thinks about the photo of the dick she found on
her phone. It already feels somewhat distant, given how
fast everything has happened today. Her mind feels like
it's been in an earthquake and then a fire, and the things

which had been close are now far away, destroyed and charred. Lucinda has never been a prostitute and yet, as a woman, she identifies with what her sister has written when she remembers her *muay thai* colleague and his twisted attempt at seduction. The way he went about it was almost as if he wanted to make it difficult for her to respond, as if the response didn't even matter; the important thing was just for him to know he had done it, even though it wasn't really a genuine advance; it was just Bruno showing himself how macho he was, how he went all the way and *really tried*, took advantage of every opportunity to seduce a woman – or rather, manipulate and mess with a woman who was not even fit to touch his muscles. Lucinda considers that if she were to make a complaint against Bruno to the academy management, what would probably happen – at the very least – is that he'd try and have it out with her, perhaps retaliate. He knew where she lived and was too proud to brush off an insult. The filter through which he observed life would not allow him to see that he had attacked first. In his head Lucinda had offended him first by deciding not to show any interest despite being fat, and then for not showing gratitude for the interest he had so generously shown her. Dialogue was impossible. It was impossible to educate that kind of man; she hadn't the slightest patience for it and wouldn't even if her sister wasn't missing and probably dead. Anyway, where could Vivi be if she wasn't dead? What could they have done with her?

Lucinda realises that she has spent her whole life trying not to make any man feel she has slighted him, because the consequences would be terrible. A whole life spent walking on eggshells. The danger of being a woman is palpable, no matter who you are, or what kind of life you lead. Tears of rage run down her face as she faces the cabin window. Viviana isn't in danger because she is a prostitute. Her ex-boyfriend is a suspect, her ex-boss in an *honest job* is a suspect, as is their father; in short, any man who had contact with Viviana and may feel slighted by her could have considered retaliation. Even if the supposed slighting made no sense, as in the case of Bruno's dick pic. I've put myself in danger, Lucinda concludes. If I hadn't toed the line, it could have been me.

She experienced this every day and didn't notice – no longer noticed. The mind is a skilled illusionist, drawing your eye to the attractive assistant while the magician escapes from being sawed in half inside a box. Lucinda's focus wanes, she can resist no longer, and finally she gives in to the memory of a silly film she and Vivi used to like, *Xanadu*, the 80s musical in which Olivia Newton-John plays the part of a roller-skating, disco-dancing Greek muse who falls in love and boosts the career of a failed graphic artist, a fit healthy boy with long hair who sometimes wears super-skimpy shorts (emphasis on the skimpy shorts). After emerging mysteriously from the cover of an LP, Olivia would skate and then disappear in a trail of neon light, leaving everyone reeling as the sounds of Electric Light Orchestra played out. Olivia's sister muses look for her everywhere in their draped dresses. The mullet-sporting graphic artist also searches for her, even in his dreams, which were animated by Don Bluth, who had left Disney and was behind some of the best-selling VHS tapes in Brazil, *The Land Before Time* and *All Dogs Go to Heaven*, as well as *Titan A.E.*, which only Vivi and Lucinda had liked out of all their friends, after watching it in the cinema. In the end, the artist in Xanadu ended up with the girl. Even though they didn't like princess movies, the message was always about the guy ending up with the girl, with his muse, his deserved reward for his courage.

Lucinda knew that Xanadu was the Asian city where Kublai Khan, founder of the Mongol empire, had a pleasure garden. Xanadu had been mentioned in an opium-inspired poem by Coleridge. It was also the name of that hypertext project which should have prefigured the internet but was never ready in time. Mere chimeras. The word 'Xanadu' fascinated her, more than anything else because in English that initial X was pronounced like a Z or an S, whereas in Portuguese it could only be *Shanadu*. Xuxa, Xanax, Xerox: everything sounded different. Xennial too, people in the space between generation X and millennials, like Lucinda, still capable of storing useless facts in their brains for moments of boredom and/or despair. A brain barren of entertainment yet still able to entertain itself with its hoarded treasure, weaving digressions, detours and inventions. Not that anyone needed it these days, with the torrent of information and non-stop entertainment and things being delivered to your home or wherever you happened to be. You had to take to the air in a plane or on a desert island to actually put that talent (was it a talent?) to use. Sometimes Lucinda thought that this was what *Lost* was about: finally being alone with your useless, uncensored thoughts.

But were they really so useless? Is it not just a different way of thinking? Could my sister be out there somewhere, also thinking about Xanadu? *Living* in Xanadu, who knows? How do I reach her? Walk into a wall? She shakes her head. It's not a good time for dreamers, with or without roller skates.

Calmer now, Lucinda accepts the packet of brazil nut cookies offered by the flight attendant. Her thoughts wander and stop at Graziane, who must have been talking to Leo Faulhaber at that very moment. Lucinda has the feeling that nothing will come of it; Graziane seemed despairing and directionless. Suddenly she wonders: why isn't Graziane in Vivi's book? Up until now Viviana hasn't mentioned her. If she and her sister are lovers, there has to be something about her in the book, doesn't there? Well, there isn't. With a simple use of the search function, Lucinda has confirmed that there is no one with the name of Graziane or Andreza. Maybe another name? But if all the names Vivi used were real…

She decides to look in the cuts.docx file. There it is.

I was in a hotel in Dubai with a Japanese guy when I heard someone talking in Portuguese. Brazilian Portuguese. The guy who was talking looked like a businessman and was vaguely familiar to me. I also noticed with a single glance that the girl he was with, silent and demure, was Brazilian too. She was really something, well fed, built, the body of a blonde goddess, strong calves. She noticed she was being watched and looked back over at me; I excused myself to my partner, and she to hers, and we went to the bathroom at the same time. 'Where are you from?' she asked. 'Rio.' 'I'm from Paraná.' And on it went. There was a football game showing, it was the 2014 world cup, Brazil were playing and no one noticed how long we took. We talked, realised our backgrounds were similar, exchanged contact details. We went back to our own tables, me with my crazy Japanese guy, showing me off and showing off his money, buying round after round. Alcohol is banned in the UEA, it's prohibited by Islam, so it's very expensive and only found in hotel bars, in theory exclusively for foreigners. The result is that some hotels are practically brothels; Emiratis go there to have their minds blown, with scantily clad women, sex for sale, alcohol which they're not used to… you've seen that, right? And this was a sports bar, there was a game on the whole time. Everything's very masculine in Dubai. I went to a mall that had a flight simulator and a dinosaur skeleton in it. It has the tallest skyscraper in the world, the first ever seven-star hotel. It's all very Arabian Nights, only with technology. That's why men love going to Dubai. Their pricks feel a mile long. They go there for the hookers; they have every kind, black, Arab, African, Russians, white as snow but controlled by the Russian mafia so you need to be smart if you want to go there, there's the threat of blackmail, extortion, other problems, best to go with a girl from somewhere else. I went with the Japanese guy, and met Grazi.

We got on really well. We formed a partnership – an exchange. We both began attending to each other's clientele. I went back to Brazil and took on more domestic clients, contacts Grazi had given me; she took advantage of my gringo clients too, not to mention the help I gave her with her English. If forcing someone to watch TV shows with English subtitles counts as helping...

Lucinda becomes aware that, really, the explanation is quite simple: her sister had removed all the most personal sections and put them in cuts.docx. She wanted to protect Lucinda and Graziane. Protect the people she loved.

If, as seems ever more likely, the whole thing is partly fictitious, this was the truth that her sister wanted to be left to history, if there was any. And, even with Vivi's distant and casual manner transplanted to these pages, Lucinda senses the passion the two feel for each other shining through. She wants to at least try to trust Graziane. In any case, she's the only other person helping her try to find her sister.

Lucinda feels a tremor and looks outside. The plane is extending its landing gear and approaching the ground.

7

LUCINDA

1979. The notary's daughter is riding the crest of the legal wave. Her head is fully screwed on and she incorporates the – at the time – brand-new feature known as a Prenuptial Agreement for Total Separation of Assets into the papers her suited, sweating groom signs immediately after the ceremony, without even reading them. Fourteen years later she hands it to her ex-husband-to-be, who had not wanted to believe in the existence of that sheet of paper until he saw it in the flesh, inside a thick plastic sheet with his signature witnessed by his father-in-law's notary, in the presence of two other lawyers. On this side of the glass table, his friend who had agreed to give him advice for mate's rates shakes his head: there isn't much you can do about it, Mauro.

In 1993 there were no camera phones nor many CCTV cameras, and so the incident in which Mauro is said to have smashed the tabletop to pieces with his fist wasn't recorded or circulated on any medium more durable than the human mind. Cássia paid for the new glass herself and instructed her lawyers to respect the wounded pride of her ex-husband to be. Even when he disappeared for three years and even when he re-emerged in Mogi das Cruzes, living with his parents, she never acted in the way you would expect a lawyer and notary's daughter to act, that is, by demanding a court order for her partner to pay child support or else that he be imprisoned for lack of compliance. All she asked was that he sign the divorce papers, which at that point he did willingly.

Mauro lives in Guarulhos now, with a new, young wife, a little daughter who's always on the go, crawling about the place, and a teenage stepdaughter who isn't back from school yet. His wife isn't back from work yet either. Holding the toddler girl in his arms he fiddles with the TV and talks to Lucinda. The way he and Lucinda speak to each other, coolly avoiding the maze of thorns which has grown around their relationship, is genuinely impressive to behold. He speaks about work, the weather, the differences between Rio and São Paulo. Even politics. Even politics is preferable to family matters.

As he talks, Lucinda takes a moment to take in how much he has aged. The same tall, stocky bearing as Lucinda, with the addition of a beer belly that she might have herself if it wasn't for the *muay thai*. His skin tone has faded a little with age. His lovely curls, which Lucinda has partly inherited, are now almost gone, and what little remains is shaved close. She notices that he is hiding his baldness by wearing a black cap with FBI written on it, which is rather off-putting to Lucinda, as if her father were playing at being a superhero at sixty. It must feel for him like a way of batting off old age, Lucinda imagines; she sees it as more of a throwback to the militarist symbols of 1980s films and TV series aimed at an older audience, one that has the ultimate effect of merely highlighting his age. But, she reasons, he still has lead in his pencil, he can still make babies – that is what his new daughter, Lucinda's half-sister, now sitting back on the table, appears to prove.

A jingling of keys causes the three faces to turn towards the door. A skinny, pale teenager with straight hair and a purple rucksack enters, shuts the door and looks up from her phone long enough to say:

'Hi.'

'Hi, Mirella. This is my oldest daughter, Lucy. Lucinda.'

'Hi,' Mirella says, with a smile that fades in record time.

'Hi,' Lucinda replies. 'Did my sister give you that phone?'

Mirella blinks, briefly startled.

'Yeah… she did.'

'I recognised the case.'

Lucinda thinks of asking if she knows who the image on the case is of, but she doesn't, because of course there is no way her father's stepdaughter could know about that 90s gem she and her sister watched in secret together on some cable channel, falling about the place in laughter and admiration. Nomi Malone, drawn as an anime character and printed onto a personalised phone case covered in pink glitter. Viviana had her own thoughts about exclusivity and had commissioned a Brazilian artist who usually did furry pornography to create that image which showed Nomi dancing semi-naked, enveloped in glitter, her hands crossed just below her face, on her breasts, like Sailor Moon when she undergoes her transformation. 'You're nuts, Vivi,' Lucinda had said, as she always said. Since her late teenage years, when she started having her own money, Viviana had always loved inventing her own fashion. Paperclips as earrings, baggy leg warmers with dungarees and clogs (a controversial look for a family lunch), the vinyl collection she had started before everyone else caught on to that trend, the choice of the name Josefel for her black cat... Lucinda came to interpret all this as a desperate cry for attention or a chaotic attempt at self-expression by someone who had, let's not forget, been diagnosed as autistic. But now Lucinda wonders if it wasn't a distraction, a 'look away, don't think I'm different from the others, I'm just a weirdo girl' thing. Hiding in plain sight with her glittery Nomi Malone–Sailor Moon.

'When did she give you that phone?'

'Around six months ago.'

'So she comes here a lot,' Lucinda says, turning towards her father.

'Of course,' Mauro replies, looking at the television, which is showing a repeat of a soap.

Lucinda looks to the door, but Mirella isn't there any more. She must have gone to her room.

Lucinda has been to Guarulhos before. But she didn't contact her father, nor did her father ever invite her to visit – unlike Viviana. She realises that, after all this time, she doesn't know him any more, doesn't know what kind of man he is, if he's still a bona fide womaniser, if he still has an explosive temper. It makes sense that he's closer to Viviana, who was too small to understand the shitty way he behaved with Cássia when they were married, the disappearances, the nights away, the doors he slammed when questioned. 'I was stuck at work,' he always claimed. Mauro was a chemist and worked for a fizzy drinks company. 'I have to do a course at the São Paulo office,' he'd announce on Thursday, and stay away until Sunday, coming home with flowers for Cássia and stickers for the girls. The final straw had been the marks he left on Cássia's arm from shaking her after, he claimed, she had driven him 'crazy with non-stop interrogations'. The body of the crime substantiating the separation of bodies. Five years old at the time, Viviana had not taken in the seriousness of the event, only heard the softened version of the story, told to the child who had been hiding in her room at the time. Perhaps that's why she was prepared to help her father now – maybe she felt he was the victim of an injustice. Or who knows, maybe she had become a victim of his violence in some way. But to get to the bottom of things Lucinda must play dumb, act understanding, ask questions.

'I was doing my sister's accounts and I saw that she occasionally transfers money into your account. Are you having financial difficulties?'

Mauro flinches before responding.

'What if I am? I don't like being short of money, I really don't, Lucinda. Viviana wanted to help me. I only asked her for help once. Then we became closer again.'

Lucinda is emphatic:

'Twice a month?'

'Is that why you came here? To rub it in my face?' He pauses, not taking his eyes off the TV. 'Look, she's been coming here ever since Clarinha was born. I thought you'd also come to visit me today; but no, you've come to rub it in my face…'

'Do you know where Vivi gets her money from?' Lucinda asks.

Mauro grimaces and says nothing.

'So you do have an idea…' Lucinda states. 'And you've never tried to interfere?'

'Who am I to poke about in her life?'

'Her father!'

Mauro closes his mouth and continues to look at the TV, offended but trying not to erupt. Lucinda says nothing more. She also looks at the TV, waiting for the tide of rage to subside. She recognises the six o'clock drama she used to watch when she was a kid, with a version of 'Sympathy for the Devil' sung by a vampire rock chick. From what she remembers, there used to be more nudity and adult content on the programme; these new versions are too concise, all cut up and lacking the juicy parts.

Her theory was that her father had blackmailed Viviana when he'd found out about her secret job. She expected nothing better from someone who had assaulted his wife, disappeared so as not to have to pay child support and then, when he reappeared, continued not to pay up. In fact, Mauro pretended not to know about Viviana, let her play with the baby and play the role of cool aunt for Mirella and, in exchange, she paid him a kind of stipend.

112

Obviously there is no way he'd kill his golden-egg-laying goose. Lucinda still thinks it possible that there could have been a lethal fight between them. But it would have been tricky for that homicidal hypothesis to have taken place in her father's house, in front of the child, with Mirella about to get back from school, phone in hand. Even so, Lucinda doesn't trust him, and is reluctant to convince herself of Mauro's innocence.

'I want to tell you something,' Mauro says, without taking his eyes off the TV. 'Remember that trip your sister took way back, to Mogi? When she came to stay with me during the holidays? She must have been fifteen or sixteen.'

'Yes, I remember.'

'If Viviana was sixteen you would have been what? Twenty? That's right, you were at university.'

'I remember, it was 2003.'

Mauro speaks in a serious, hushed tone.

'She went to Mogi to have an abortion.'

Lucinda opens her mouth and glares. Mauro looks at Lucinda, observes her reaction and continues.

'She called me one weekend explaining that Cássia was turning a blind eye to everything, as long as she kept doing well at school and avoided getting sick or pregnant. And she was doing badly at school that year, it seems she was skiving too much, and she'd found out that she was pregnant. She said that the condom split. She said that if she asked her mother for money for an abortion, Cássia would lock her up and throw away the key. And it was a real possibility, don't you think? We all know what Cássia's like. Vivi told me she was broke, that her mother

113

kept everything she earned. So she came up with this plan to come to Mogi in the July holidays, in theory to see me. In practice it was to… get rid of the kid. I paid for it. The trip and the procedure. Today I have a small daughter and Vivi helps me. She helps her sister. And I'm grateful.'

Lucinda breaks eye contact with her father to process this information. She had interpreted her sister's trip to Mogi in a completely different way. She was twenty at the time, in her third year of university. The university had begun a long strike, which coincided with the split of her college band, ultimately owing to her relationship with the singer and guitarist – who, she had discovered, cheated on her without hesitation. So while her sister had taken a 'holiday' with their father, she had stayed at home sobbing, listening to Radiohead on repeat (by then *Kid A* and *Amnesiac* had both been released and the towers had fallen) and feeling rejected on all sides. Even now she knew the real reason behind her sister's trip, the sense of rejection endured.

'Did it never occur to you to invite me, so that I wouldn't feel like total shit?' Lucinda asks.

'I did, but you didn't even call me on my birthday.'

'Neither did you on mine.'

'Yes I did!' Mauro shouts, slapping his thigh and making the baby look up at him from her squishy playmat. Mauro stops for a moment, to contain himself, then continues, more calmly now. 'You always said to say you weren't there, you think I don't know that? You wanted nothing to do with me.'

Lucinda tries to swallow her rage. It's true, she had been very hard on her father as a teenager. He had kept trying. Once again, the blame was hers. But she bore it. That was all she was good for... to take a beating from life, to have to deal with all the shit other people had started. Now her father was offended.

'You mean you came here to accuse me. To mock me.'

Lucinda notices a shadow moving on the floor, the corridor light revealing that Mirella has been lurking there, listening in. She decides to get to the core of this mutual self-pity session, looks into her father's eyes and says:

'That wasn't my intention, Dad, it wasn't. It just... came out. We can talk about our relationship another time. I came because Viviana's gone missing.'

'Missing?' At last he shows some interest. That or he's a brilliant actor.

'She's gone missing. She said she was travelling and asked me to look after her plants and cat. It's been around a day since she's read any messages on her phone or answered a call. I only found out she'd come here because I checked her location on her computer.'

'You don't know where she is?'

'No, that's the problem. The last trace of her on her phone is near here... just after she came to see you yesterday.'

'Couldn't she just be busy in a way that means she can't get in touch?'

'A whole day without any news, without even turning on her phone? I can't believe that would happen because of work. Besides that, she missed a date with a friend and didn't let her know. If Vivi had gone somewhere with no signal she'd have at least let me know. I don't think she's forgotten.'

'And you gave me that whole spiel instead of telling me straight away that my daughter's gone missing?' Now he was grandiosely saying *my daughter, my daughter*. 'Have you spoken to the police?'

'Yes. In Rio.'

'And they did nothing?'

'Nothing. I called the hospital and morgues. No one knows anything. I'm scared it's a kidnapping.'

'She drove here. Did they take the car?'

'Was it hired?'

'I think so. It was grey, basic model.'

'Do you know which company?'

'No idea.'

'Oh my God.' Lucinda starts to cry, before wiping her face with two hand movements.

Mauro looks at Lucinda in silence, the baby back in his lap.

'I'm going to take a look at the place where her signal vanished. Want to come with me?' Lucinda asks.

'On the motorway?'

'Yeah, maybe there's some sign, a clue. Her abandoned car…'

'I would come, Lucinda, but… I need to watch Clarinha.'

'Bring her.'

'To the middle of a highway?' Mauro looks at Lucinda. 'I'm trying to be responsible.'

'Sure.'

'I'd leave her with Mirella but she says she doesn't like children.'

'Sure.' Lucinda is already standing up.

'Hold on, let me talk to Mirella,' he says. 'I'll come.'

8

LUCINDA

But he didn't. Seeing her father going against his will, Lucinda dispensed with him. Mauro followed her to the door, keen at least to show her the best way of getting out of the city. Lucinda said she preferred to use GPS but he insisted, accusing her of being stubborn. This was his region, he knew everything around him, how could she not want his advice. What impressed her was how he felt authorised to put his foot down in the name of uncalled-for pride, even at a time like this; and, in his mind, she wouldn't be allowed the same behaviour, not even when faced with his paternal 'should I stay or should I go?' antics. As Mauro harangued her, the baby cried in his lap.

Lucinda just shot a sullen glance in his direction, one that carried all the weight of that day's events. He stayed quiet. Then, to save his pride, she said calmly that the only reason she'd rather use GPS was so that she wouldn't go beyond the point at which Viviana's signal had disappeared, which was right at the exit from the city, and that it really wasn't safe for Clarinha to go, that he really did need to stay with the girl, that she understood. He nodded.

They are both adults now, she thinks. Two total fucking bores, with short fuses and a few genes in common. But at least they have matured a little bit. A tiny bit.

Now, stationary at a light that can't be skipped, staring at an advert on a news-stand, she remembers how it all started. The moment everything started going wrong. The day she went to audition for the part of a teenage presenter with Viviana and her sister unwittingly stole the show, even though she was only twelve. The starting point of a career sustained by image, by social affectation, by packaging yourself like a product. That couldn't be good for your head. Cássia shouldn't have allowed it. But she had.

The clock shows that it's already past six in the evening. Lucinda merges onto the Fernão Dias highway and stays in the right lane, driving as slowly as possible while checking the GPS on her phone, held in place by a clamp on the dashboard. Suddenly, a chat balloon pops up on the screen accompanied by a chirpy noise that repeats three times. She doesn't recognise the face on the messenger app profile. She reaches out her finger, clicks on the balloon and skims through the message. Immediately after, she signals and stops in the lay-by. The problem wasn't messing around with the phone while she was driving, but the fear of driving past the point where Vivi had disappeared.

Mirella had added Lucinda on Facebook and written to her saying that she hadn't had time to show her but that when Viviana had given her the old phone she had found some photos still stored on it. Did Lucinda want to see them? Would it help? 'Yes,' Lucinda replies, 'please send them.' By offering the photos, Mirella was admitting to having listened in on the conversation between Lucinda and her father (Lucinda already knew this), seen possibly compromising photos of Vivi, taken them from the phone's memory and kept them for herself when she could have just reformatted the device when she was given it as a gift. Now she was sending them to Lucinda to help even though she risked appearing to admire Viviana, a capital crime for a teenager. Doubtless Viviana had inspired a girl crush in her stepsister, with her cosmopolitan model glamour, her whole *when I lived in Asia* spiel... How little she knew, the poor thing. Or maybe she knew a good deal.

'There's these ones,' Mirella writes, and immediately sends her an assortment of loose photos, the kinds that are left behind in hidden folders after you think you've wiped the phone before passing it on. The majority are old. The first of the bunch is a photo of Viviana's entire body, accompanied by Graziane and an Asian girl, the three of them in pencil dresses standing in front of a mirror, all made-up, a force to be reckoned with. If looks could kill. The background suggests somewhere abroad, a bar-restaurant, probably in a hotel. Then photos of sunsets, of restaurants and bottles of wine that her sister must have particularly enjoyed during her wanderings. Finally, some more photos of Grazi and Vivi together, alone and less made-up this time. Selfies apparently taken during their time off, many of them bathed in that mystical late-afternoon light. In one of them Vivi's eyes are half shut and her face is glued to Grazi's. It's the first time Lucinda has seen Graziane so close up, so shorn of artifice, and she has a beautiful, pale, noble Slavic face, with a hint of Clarice Lispector about it. Prominent cheekbones, full blonde hair, curling at the tips. Her bright, almond eyes complementing Viviana's. In one photo Grazi is alone, wearing shorts, hugging one of her legs on a beach chair in the sun. The photo has obviously been taken, lovingly, by Viviana.

'Thanks Mirella,' Lucinda types. 'Helped a lot.' And she gets back on the road. Lucinda feels a bit bad for having been so curt with Mirella, for having dismissed her so quickly. From a purely practical perspective she could at least have asked her if Viviana had gone out alone in her car yesterday, if she had seen her at home, that kind of thing. But she could ask later, if she still felt it was important. Lucinda thinks she's getting good at this, at investigating, refining her methods. Now she's managing to combine threads of clues into coherent possibilities. For example: it couldn't have been a simple case of mugging or robbery, because her sister's bank accounts show no withdrawals after her disappearance. Lucinda has the feeling she's getting somewhere.

The last sign of life shown by Viviana, a blue line ending in a dot, was just after a factory that makes bathroom accessories. The GPS isn't 100 per cent precise, so Lucinda signals, stops in the lay-by and, putting her blinkers on, gets out of the car holding the phone. On the screen she magnifies the end of Viviana's journey and the dot indicating her own position on the map as much as possible. Perhaps the exact location of the disappearance is a little after or maybe just above that line, but she's more or less in the right place to start looking. She can't see any abandoned vehicles there; if there had been one it might have already been towed and returned to the hire company.

Six forty p.m., she checks. Even though it's high summer the sun is almost on the horizon, and this area will start to get dark soon. Lucinda starts walking quickly, looking at the ground. She looks at the flower bed next to the lay-by: it can hardly be called a flower bed, containing only dying grass; mostly you can just see clayey soil that has slid down the slope into it. The remainders of puddles show that it has rained the day before. If Viviana's car had gone onto the side of the road, there might have been tyre marks imprinted on that path, but the curb is too high for a car to get onto it. It also isn't a place where people set foot all that often: it isn't near any junctions, paths or residential areas. When she walks in the direction of traffic towards the end of the overpass and the factory, she sees no marks on the lay-by or the curb. As she walks back she is paying maximum attention to the earth in the flower bed, with its sparse gravel and scraps of grass. She thinks she must look crazy, but still she goes up and down the lay-by three times, taking in the differences between shadow and light on that red earth, without walking on it. Finally, she *sees*.

Some slightly different-looking shadows in the middle of that almost dry soil.

Lucinda gets up onto the curb and sticks her neck out.

There are bare footprints on the soil leading to a series of depressions – the weight of a body being dragged? Signs of struggle? She thinks she sees part of a splayed hand, the opened fingers of someone who had fallen on the ground – or was pushed. There are little heaps of earth, she imagines, formed perhaps by a woman's kicking feet. Her sister always drove barefoot; because she wouldn't give up her heels, she'd leave her shoes to one side, on the floor of the passenger seat. In the soil, she sees footsteps from a bigger shoe, leather, a man's, next to delicate toes which had walked on tiptoes and out of plumb. Dragged? Viviana has been kidnapped. By someone who is experienced enough to turn off her phone at the first opportunity, so there are no traces.

Lucinda looks in one direction, then the other. No security cameras nearby. Not even around the factory. She begins taking photos of the signs before they disappear. Then she takes a video of the terrain along the lay-by, narrating in a faltering voice. She makes sure to test the phone signal by sending the video to Graziane. The video gets sent. She thinks for a while, then sends the video to the WhatsApp that the cop at the Botafogo station gave her, explaining what it is, including the case number, and sending her location. Then Lucinda goes over to the disturbed soil and looks at it, fearful of finding blood. But there's no blood there, at least not that she can see. Maybe her sister is still alive, she thinks.

Trying not to think about what might be happening to Viviana if she is alive, Lucinda photographs the splayed handprints in the soil, the signs of what she thinks must have been a fight. Turning around, she positions herself right above the clearest men's shoe print and also takes a few photos. It's a flat sole, with a square tip, not remarkable in any other way. As this isn't a cop show, the police are never going to find out who owns the shoe by analysing the individual fibres found in that soil, which could only have come from a specific factory in this or that city, nor from the remains of the unique soil they might have found. The police would never undertake that kind of investigation. Lucinda balances on one foot and raises her folded knee, comparing her foot size with that of the male footprint: they are both 39. It must be a short man, Lucinda thinks. Maybe I could take him.

At this point her phone rings. It's Graziane.

'Lucinda?' she says, her voice quivering. 'Help me. I've just received a message from Vivi. But it's for you.'

PART II

VIVIANA

I like silence. This isn't silence: I can hear every single cricket, every cicada, every owl hoot. Then morning comes, and with it the dawn chorus. Infernal racket.

It's so unfair. I never asked to be this self-conscious. As a girl you're always made to come and greet visitors, let yourself be touched and prodded, and your shyness gets knocked out of you; this is what they call 'overcoming shyness' or simply 'learning some etiquette'. But it's not shyness, it's simply a desire to take in the present while also finding it difficult, because the present is a complex thing. There's so much information to take in, and your presence in the world only adds more information, and you're unable to ignore that information. You get up onto the stage, red in the face, and act, without slipping up, until the show's over. You sing and dance as if you were alone when in fact you're performing in front of the whole school. You act. The social pressure becomes background noise; to survive you learn to choose some channels and mute the others. The channel's still there, but you've learnt to ignore it and its effects. You become immune to the bullying and do what you can, trying to extract only the good from each experience, like a purified elixir.

But it's a deal with the devil. People stop calling you names but still consider you cold, withdrawn, odd. Too self-sufficient for your own good. They're afraid of you. As if you were some sort of psychopath, which is precisely what they call you behind your back.

And sometimes, scared and exhausted, you even end up running away from yourself. Like a weak heart, my brain, completely drained from so much social/antisocial strain, suddenly throws in the towel, and I drift away from wherever my body happens to be. Part of me loses consciousness while the rest stays alert.

For example, I'll drift away in the middle of an interesting story I'm telling someone because I've begun to interrogate myself: have I said enough yet to move on to the next part? What *is* the next relevant part? Why was I even telling this story? Why did I think it was important to mention it? Is me telling this story, in such minute detail, to this particular person at this specific moment in time, really so important for the universe? Once this process has begun I need to make a gargantuan effort not only to pick up where I left off but simply to summon the *motivation* to do so, look at the person (who by this time is already staring at me like I'm mad) and conclude my thoughts. It happens without warning; I drift far away and there's no way of stopping it. Instead of becoming more self-conscious, the anxiety brought on by being reminded that I have a physical body and that I'm there, taking up space, talking to another body, makes me become self-unconscious: I take leave of both myself and the person I'm talking to. I fly off to a calmer place, my own personal church, and a voice tells me that all is vanity, one great big *so what?* Like a hole in a bucket, I simply watch the water drain out through that funnel, neither happy nor sad, doing nothing and not wishing to do anything. The water is my ego, I figure. I can watch the other person's reactions change millisecond by millisecond, passing through annoyance, boredom, attempting to hide what they're feeling, wondering what my problem is, if I've got something against them, if I'm on ecstasy, if I'm not feeling well or if I've got a screw loose (that must be it, they conclude), while I try to make myself be there again, *come back down.*

The strange thing is that after experiencing this absence I do always manage to take up the thread again and look back at everything that happened. I'm thirty-one years old and I still suffer from these attacks. They come without warning and I can't stop them or dodge them. I get lost, then I come back. Generally, the people who witness this happening to me already know I act weird sometimes, and they think it's OK, what's the harm, it's an interesting story and they want to hear what happens. This helps me learn about normal people, but it never fixes me for good, or turns me into one of them.

I overanalyse things. That's what I was told in therapy. I was also told that I have 'mild experiences of depersonalisation' and 'disassociation'. At school they said I was autistic. One psychologist at the time confirmed that diagnosis, and said I had Asperger's. Others said it was attention deficit disorder, or dysthymia. I don't know what I have. I look at all those diagnoses and don't recognise myself in any of them. It's a shop full of things I don't need.

None of us wants to feel horrible. We assume that everyone works hard not to *be* horrible so that they can fulfil this social goal. But people who don't feel much manage to attain the level of not *feeling*: they can *be* as horrible as they like, because they don't *feel* they are. Like psychopaths and sociopaths.

I know I can come across as lacking empathy. So much so that sometimes I convince myself. Recognising this is what allows me not to be sentimental about myself, and it's what is allowing me to remain sanguine in the kind of situation in which I now find myself, imprisoned in an isolated house somewhere in the countryside. I don't know if it's Minas Gerais, São Paulo state, maybe even the far north of Rio state. I know the car that brought me here seemed to be going up rather than down the map, and I know it's freezing in the way only ranches can be.

I know that my apparent lack of interest in everything around me can appear to come from pure coldness. But I'm not trying to appear cold and distant, nor do I take pleasure from it: I really am quite often like that. To protect myself I select which information I allow in, but I also need to pay attention to the correct facets of reality. And to acknowledge this I need to police myself, train myself, and that's tough. I need to look outwards and pay constant attention – the most difficult thing in the world for someone who's already overburdened. It's easy to get sloppy. That's why I'm not always aware if I'm being horrible or not, even with myself, which is why someone once called me a psychopath, and that upset me because I do have feelings, lots of them. But people don't see that because

I forget to recognise and display these feelings, even to myself. I've learnt to muffle the feelings somewhat, including to my own ears, because there are too many and the majority never get out from inside me. I end up choking on them. Besides, if I was a psychopath, I'd never have let other people be horrible to me, which I do, because I don't understand the nuances in their behaviour (at least not until it's too late). I can force myself to understand social signals, and from so much forcing I end up becoming more astute than the ones who've never had to practise. The problem is keeping up the training, and this is a training regime that will never end.

It's not coldness. But I must admit that sometimes it can be a good substitute for it.

So, at moments like this, we work with what we've got.

I analyse.

To call Davi a psychopath would be to give him too much credit. Davi is Truly Normal, an average man capable of horrible things, who adjusts to situations by externalising his guilt and blurring his own narrative so he doesn't have to take responsibility for his actions. The feelings are there; they're what he uses to muddy the waters in his head. As for that henchman of his, I have no idea. But he seems perfectly capable of killing.

The current narrative in Davi's head is that it's dangerous to let me go right now because I might go to the police and report him for maltreatment, kidnapping and false imprisonment. I've got visible marks on my body that would back up my claims. And he doesn't even know my mother's a lawyer. He wants to let the marks fade so

131

I don't have any evidence against him. The henchman disagrees.

Every now and then, Davi comes over and strokes my arm or my face, as if he were giving me a reward. Other times he stops reading suddenly and sits there watching me, evaluating my natural, make-up-free features. The only colour on my face is from the scratches and bruises. He seems to be satisfied, confirming my beauty to himself; I am indeed an object worthy of his interest. He seems relieved by the distraction of looking outside for a moment.

I feel like a little bird. He gives me bits of food in napkins, chunks of bread, whole pieces of fruit or something pre-prepared so he doesn't need to give me a knife or glass. For lunch I had a tuna sandwich. I drink water from a tin mug. I could attack him, bite the hand that feeds me, but there's no point, I've already tried. If I'm going to try again I need to save the element of surprise for a more suitable moment.

For now, I need to pretend my anger has subsided, that I regret having broken his heart – several times – that he's really cool and I'm only now realising it. But I mustn't exaggerate, or he won't believe me.

I should have noticed at the time. The car rammed into the boot at the exit from the city, just after I had joined the motorway and got stuck behind some grandad who was driving slowly even for the slow lane. I hadn't put my belt on yet, and though the collision didn't cause me to fly into the wheel or activate the airbag, it did stun me. I stopped in the lay-by and so did he; groaning, he got out of his Corolla and came walking along the lay-by towards me, wearing a white dress shirt and black trousers. He had a bald patch. I remember thinking: 'That's someone's driver. Is he insured or is he going to try to pull a fast one?' I opened the window a tiny bit. 'Are you OK?' he asked. 'Yes,' I nodded from behind the glass. 'Are you insured?' I asked. He pointed to his ear to communicate that he couldn't hear me because of the noise from the road; I lowered the window a bit further and he pulled out a gun. I motioned to start the car and he grabbed my neck with his free hand, waved the gun in my face and said, 'Open the door, slut. Come on, open up, bitch.' I did what he said. He had to fight to drag me to his car, pulling me by my arm, my hair, me shouting the whole time as the cars flew by, but if anyone saw anything they pretended they hadn't. At some point I wriggled free and ran a couple of metres in the mud towards the wire fence by the roadside, but he caught up and knocked me over. He forced me into the Corolla and threw me onto the passenger seat with my hands tied. Then, somewhat ironically, he did up my seat belt. I resisted, which earned me two painful slaps to the face and a punch in the stomach, which stopped me in my tracks because I simply couldn't breathe. I was all scratched up, covered in mud, my scalp hurt. He contemplated his work and chuckled:

'Easy there, I'm not going to do anything. You're special. You need to arrive in one piece.'

Then, as if to protect me from the cold, he threw a jacket over me, concealing my tied hands. He left my rented car where it was, moved off in the Corolla and we took the route towards the city, whizzing down a series of main roads I'd never seen before. He didn't use the GPS, so he must have known the way by heart. He knew which spots to avoid, the most brightly lit stretches and the busiest parts, where he'd be forced to drive slowly. The piece of shit had a toll tag and a full tank, and the tinted windows were as dark as night; I soon lost all hope of attracting someone's attention while we were stationary. He had obviously planned the whole thing, and by the looks of it he was working for someone else. But who? I thought it was worth a try.

'Where are you taking me?' I asked.

'Shut up.' I obeyed.

Night fell. Soon it was so dark that all we could see were the lights of the other cars and trucks, and the trees framing the leaden sky. He drove carefully, with no music or any sound at all, protected by the all-encompassing darkness. We entered a hilly section. Some stretches of the road ran along the edge of the cliff, with insufficient light to start with and then none at all, only the eternal third line marked on the tarmac ahead of us, and on some bends we could make out, through the thick forest, specks of light moving much further down, the lamps of cars making their way along another stretch of the road. We'd pass through that part shortly, I calculated. And we did. Then there were more and more roads, for nearly three hours, and I didn't relax for a single second. Road signs indicating the exits for cities I'd never heard of came and went, saints' names or long indigenous words that didn't help me orient myself one bit. We passed a restaurant called Cantinho Mineiro. Were we in Minas? I tried to remember my geography lessons: Serra da Mantiqueira, Serra da Canastra, Serra da Bocaina. I tried to remember where each one was, but instead names of minerals I'd learnt in fifth grade came to me: gneiss, hematite, feldspar. To calm myself down I began to think of a mineral for every letter of the alphabet: aluminium, bauxite, carbon. Sitting there imagining my fate was wearing me out and beginning to intoxicate me, and my mind made an escape from my captive state, even if it was only to play alphabet games in my head. And I let it, lacking both the strength and the will to intervene. Uranium, vanadium, wardite, zircon. I couldn't think of any minerals beginning with X or Y. The last few letters of the alphabet were mysterious and difficult. Algebra always used x, y or z. And the neutral gender: latinx, amigxs. I thought about *The X-Files*, which I used to watch with Lucinda, both of us pretending only to be in love with Mulder. That was the first time I heard the word 'abduction', a term for when someone is kidnapped by aliens and vanishes, which made me think of the word 'ravish', which is an archaic way of saying 'rape'. In the final seasons of *The X-Files* we discovered that Mulder's sister had been kidnapped by aliens, who had made several clones of her, and that made me remember the Brazilian drama *The Clone*. As well as being about a human clone and some Moroccan Muslims, *The Clone* was the story of drugged-up Mel, who drank perfume and drove parents to despair, including real ones: even my mother began to inspect Lucinda and me far more often and rigorously, which had the effect of accelerating our departure from the family home – to different houses, because by then we were older and it was too late for us. Mel's look resembled a clubber, all tight T-shirts and metallic jackets, perhaps inspired by Renton from *Trainspotting*, which had recently come out at the time. I sighed as I recalled young, heroin-chic Ewan McGregor, going cold turkey locked up in his room, watching a baby crawl across the ceiling... this in turn ignited a memory of the ultimate villain, Nazaré Tedesco, kidnapping another woman's baby, always acting crazy and making a big scene on public transport. I came out of my reverie when the car began to judder; we were on an earth track now. I realised we were close. Close to the end? I tried to prepare myself for whatever was coming, which was obviously impossible. Who is ever prepared for rape, for death or the torture that comes before death? There was no escape now.

I remembered films I shouldn't have watched: *A Serbian Film, Requiem for a Dream, Saw, Paradise Lost, Martyrs*. I was shaking all over, I could hardly breathe. Everything was slowly turning white, from the corners in. My body wanted to faint, from hunger and from fear, but I forced myself to stay conscious. I wouldn't give up without a fight. A single dot of light got closer – I figured we were on a ranch or farm – and as we got closer and saw the porch and eaves of a farmhouse my suspicions were confirmed. My brain was in a similar state, with a single light on inside, right in the middle, the pilot flame. After parking in front of the house the man got out, slammed the door shut and left me there, tied up, my back against the main door. I turned my neck and watched him enter the house; despite being tied up I undid the belt and tried the door handles – locked. There was only a bunch of papers inside the glovebox; he'd taken the gun. The man came back a little later, accompanied by a face that I recognised with some effort and no small amount of surprise: I wasn't as screwed as I had imagined. Or was I even more screwed?

Davi. Davi had been with me just once, months earlier, in peculiar circumstances. I had used my Rio apartment to see clients for a few days, instead of the aparthotel, which had a leak. I remembered him pausing as he removed my clothes, contemplating the bookshelves in the living room and asking if I had read 'all of them'. I smiled. 'Most of them,' I replied. We fucked and chatted, loafing about in domestic comfort, and it was obvious he was impressed by my conversation and even more impressed when I put on his shirt and, all authoritative, went to make coffee for us without even asking him if he wanted any. I was very much at ease; it was my house after all. I took great care to create that atmosphere of intimacy, the kind of experience that yields a second and third hook-up. Davi spent several hours in the apartment, scoping out what we had in common (from Russian classics to graphic novels) and I think I passed the test; he fucked me again and paid what I asked without complaining.

After that day he kept sending me messages on my phone, inviting me to all kinds of hipster things, from craft beer bars to graphic novel launches. Always as if he was already going and had only thought to invite me at the last moment. There was no mention in his messages of the advance financial agreement which more experienced clients know is standard practice for someone on the game, unless it didn't need to be mentioned or had become unnecessary due to the kind of relationship of mutual trust which is established over time, after repeated hook-ups. We definitely weren't at that stage yet. Had I showed up I'd doubtless have found Davi surrounded by friends of his age and social class. I'd be the rare bird on show, to be rubbed in their faces; I'd be shown off as his model friend; he'd make it obvious we were fucking and I wouldn't get a penny for such a monumental waste of time. He must have assumed that his attractiveness, social contacts and family wealth would be enough for me. But they weren't. I never took him up on any of the dates he proposed. Fucking a rich man for free goes against my professional principles. When he found out I also spent time in São Paulo he began inviting me to things there. As his attempts to establish a different kind of relationship between us floundered, he began offering me gifts of a cultural nature. First he'd send me photos of books by authors he admired: 'Do you know this one? Want me to get it for you? There's this limited edition…' I tuned out. Sometimes I'll accept presents as barter when the guy has sugar daddy vibes, but I don't need anyone to buy me books! At the very least it has to be jewellery. Davi thought he knew me well, when really he was investing in a kind of fetish – possessing a girl who was immersed in the world of 'male culture', that is, his culture – and I had a feeling that it could be dangerous. Not to mention boring.

It was a hook-up, but he wanted it to be a relationship.

I had been dragged here on the orders of a guy I didn't even want to talk to any more; he must have been wanting something more than sex to take such a risk. A girlfriend? Only if I was a paid girlfriend; if it was a matter of my playing that part, I could do it perfectly well, and he had the money. But from the looks of it he didn't want to have to pay.

How ironic. As an Exotic Beauty I was always the one everyone wanted a taste of, but never to be seen with on a date. I ended up deciding to monetise it because I was fed up with people benefiting from being associated with me whilst at the same time undervaluing me. I carved out my niche: the resourceful exotic girl who can romp with elegance, a kind or pre-watershed bad girl, a little bit crazy *pero no mucho*. Then I spent some time abroad, embodying universal cliches such as the schoolgirl in their local variations, charging less than was ideal because of wily middlemen.

Yet despite all this I never inserted much of my personality or cultural tastes into that character, partly to protect myself, partly because of my aversion to fetishes for nerd/hipster girls, but mainly because nobody wants to hear about a cultured bad girl. It would complicate the message too much. Even the book I'm writing now is a careful and partial view of my life in the sex trade. The reason for publishing it would be to retire from the profession, something I've been feeling more and more inclined to do. My plan was not to give away anything essential in the book: no talking about my girlfriend, my mental issues or my cultural preferences, just juicy anecdotes, marketing lessons and appeals to be less narrow-minded. That would be quite enough. Yet the more I wrote, the more I doubted I'd ever be able to finish and publish it, confined as I was to the labyrinths I myself had created. Vívian's outlook in the book, which without fully admitting it was based on my personality, generated prerequisites and interdependencies that were different from mine, which I couldn't ignore and was unable to develop, forming an incoherent, volatile personality. However much I claimed that those two-bit memoirs were only to make money, I had a certain pride in being the way I was, in how I had constructed myself in life, and I worried about the quality of the writing – which is why I was close to giving up on all of that and plotting another retirement route.

But before I could decide, Davi appeared. What an idiot. I wondered how he could have found me, what had impelled him to seek out a professional and why me specifically. Maybe he didn't know where to find women after finishing university, women up for no-strings sex, since he wasn't ready to marry yet (and in that world of wealth you had to get married). He was always into the latest trend anyway, but he wanted something that made him stand out from the masses. He went out with groups of friends, but the best thing was to be alone. Had he gone to a massage parlour with some friends, and then started looking for escorts by himself?

Then I came along. And I thought: so beautiful, so sexy, so dumb. Separating my feelings as always to stop them controlling me: the serotonin of the orgasm, the endorphins of being on top, the oxytocin of having fucked the same person twice. That way I'm only benefiting. And I still get paid.

When Davi saw me, all beaten and bruised in the car, he looked apprehensive. He didn't say anything to the tough who had kidnapped me, doubtless some yes-man who worked for his father the rancher, but he opened the passenger door and spoke to me: 'Viviana.' My real name. So he had been investigating me. Shit.

'Viviana, please, forgive me.' He looked at me in horror and anguish. 'I didn't want this.'

I looked at him, hands tied on my lap, and said:

'Davi.'

'It was César's idea,' he said, nodding in the direction of the man who had kidnapped me. Davi looked very serious, hoping I would believe him. 'It was his idea. I'd never have let him if I'd known.'

I couldn't decide if it was time for me to say something yet, including asking him to untie me. I was still weighing him up, trying to discover how long he'd let this crazy situation go on for. I jiggled my hands around on my lap.

'Let me untie you,' he said, trying to undo the knot with his nails. He couldn't. 'There's some scissors inside, come on.'

I didn't move from where I was. 'Come on,' he insisted. César, who was keeping his distance, took a step forward. I understood. Resting my tied hands on my knees, I got up and left the car. I walked, in little geisha steps, my tied hands impeding movement, feet frozen on the earthen ground, then the wooden floor, into a big, old, colonial-style living room. The floor was done with hydraulic tiles, the kind that cost fifty reais a piece. They made me sit on a sofa. No one was getting any scissors.

Davi was annoyed. Annoyed because, I deduced, that situation didn't fit with his fantasies: I still hadn't declared my love for him nor wept and begged for pity. I was barely disguising the fury I felt, which even trumped the fear lying beneath. César continued to stand there, short and solid, surveying the scene. Davi walked back and forth across the room, the classic worried businessman.

'She's all bruised, C,' Davi said at last, leaning on the soft back of a rustic sofa. 'Did you hit her?'

Did you hit her? Good God! The worst thing was having to witness this condescending scene, as if I was incapable of noticing the terrible acting, the clichés. I was beginning to feel more angry than scared.

'She wouldn't come willingly,' said César.

'Viviana, my plan was for him to talk to you, convince you to come. Not this…'

'Get that guy away from me,' I said.

'Calm down,' Davi continued. 'I know you must be scared. Take it easy, we'll untie you. But let's talk first.'

'The three of us?'

'The two of us. César lives and works here. I can't kick him out. But he's going to leave us alone now,' he said, stroking my face.

I flinched from his touch. Maybe I shouldn't have been in such a hurry to get rid of the other guy. Davi had the air of a prince, including the height and a tendency towards insanity, but even so it seemed better to take him on alone than to face both him and his henchman.

'I'll talk to you,' I said, as if it was my decision, 'but not in front of him.'

'Or while tied up,' I thought, but I wouldn't say that just yet, not in front of César. I berated myself for having put off those self-defence classes Lucinda wanted me to take. Even though I could see how much stronger my sister had gotten since she'd started her *muay thai* classes, I got comfortable and let my ego convince me that in any adverse situation I'd be capable of turning the tables just using my intellect, my ability to read patterns.

'Don't worry, darling, I'm going,' César said, baring his teeth at me in an aggressive smile. He nodded at Davi and left through the front door. I heard the car driving away. My bag, phone and charger were in it. Shit.

Davi took me to the tiled bathroom, sat me down on the toilet lid and began to patch me up – without untying my hands. I had a scratch on my forehead, which he disinfected without putting on a plaster, before attending to the scratches and bruises on my arm, all of which I could see when I turned my neck, which also hurt. I was all dirty with dried mud from when I'd tried to escape in the layby. There must have been bruises beneath my trousers too. My shoulders and back hurt from the tension. And my stomach.

'This rope's cutting into my wrist,' I said.

Davi had just cleaned my left arm with a wet cloth. Without saying anything, he picked up some nail scissors from the case on his lap and tried, unsuccessfully, to cut the rope.

'Wait,' he said, 'I'll be back. But you… you must promise…' He turned the palm of his hand towards me. 'Stay there.'

Davi took out the key from the old, dark wooden door, and locked me in from the outside, taking the key. I got up and went over to the open tilting window. It was too high, like the ceilings themselves. I opened the cupboard above the sink: I found cotton wool and a toilet roll stored in a crochet holder. Another free-standing Formica cupboard in the corner was locked. I went back to the toilet seat and sat down again.

If you're a competent hooker, it doesn't take long for you to weigh up your client and sketch a kind of psychological profile of him, finding out what he likes in bed even if he doesn't know it himself. I desperately employed this skill at that moment, speculating by bringing together what little I knew about Davi. In the past Graziane had had a few appointments with Davi's father, a rancher of mixed ethnicity who only liked blondes and paid good money for undepilated naturals. Davi's mother must have also looked like that because Davi was white and a dark shade of blond. His father was conservative in a particularly Brazilian way, of course: his escapades had to be tolerated and, whatever happened, his daughter-in-law had to have light skin. Davi's infatuation with me, a woman who was far from blonde, white or pure, was the opposite of what his parents expected from him – and Freud explains the rest. But if the henchman had gone to the extreme of kidnapping me for Davi, did that mean I was better than nothing? That question remained unanswered.

The family wealth came from monocultures and cattle farming, but Davi did not resemble your typical wealthy rancher in any way; either he wanted to stand out or he really was too different to fit in. From the conversation we had during my first appointment with him, I knew that he had an entirely urban group of friends and that he had dropped out of college a few times, eventually graduating in business studies from a private university. Searching my memory, I remembered that Graziane had mentioned that her regular client, the rancher, had a 'problematic' son, who didn't have 'a head for business' and had once been sectioned, either for drug abuse or some psychiatric problem, it wasn't clear. And Davi was an only child, at least officially. Too fragile for everyday life, his father paying for everything. Perhaps now his family was pressuring him to have a girlfriend, a wife, a 'normal' life.

When we gather references for potential clients, what we're really doing is protecting ourselves: we want to know if the guy has already slapped some other girl about, if he's tried to rip people off; in other words, we want to see his rap sheet. Davi's past had escaped me. But I had also had issues with mental health and recreational drugs. Thinking about it now, it was clear that the concept of a dangerous alpha male resided in Davi's head, even though it did not match with reality. That was the danger, the real danger. The women he considered acceptable weren't forming a queue behind him, the sexy and cultured girls of his fantasies, girls full of attitude whom he'd hope to show off to his friends and who would redeem him in his father's eyes. Besides the pent-up frustration and rage, he was visibly depressed.

He came back a short while later, holding a knife. A basic cooking knife, with a flat blade, the kind you use to cut meat and onions or stick into a banana tree to cast a spell on someone. Without saying anything, Davi walked over to me, a grim expression on his face. The strange thing was I didn't feel afraid. I remember having thought that his sombre air had to be a sign of his discomfort with the situation. I immediately wondered if I was succumbing to Stockholm syndrome.

Davi came closer, crouched down in front of me and slowly brought the tip of the knife to the middle of my wrists, slipping it under the centre. The knife was sharp. After a few attempts the rope came completely undone and fell away, slowly unravelling from the sides of my wrists. My skin burned, worn down by the friction.

He began massaging my wrists and it burned even more. I pulled them back and started to get up. He got up with me, grabbed my arm and stopped me.

'I've untied you, but you're not leaving here.'

'I'm only going to the sink to wash my wrist.' But I didn't, he kept holding me.

'Listen up' – he was still holding me – 'I don't like what César did to you. It wasn't what I wanted.'

The same old spiel. And all the while he was gripping my arm.

'Doesn't César work for you?'

'He does…' he said, scornfully. 'He's almost like a brother.'

'Then he did you a favour.'

David let go of my arm and went all pensive, looking downwards.

'You have to believe me. I didn't want this.'

'Prove it, then. Let me go. Let me leave.'

'I can't. You're all bruised, they'll think it was me. I could go to jail.'

'You really think I'm going to go and talk to the police? You know very well what I do for a living.'

'I know, Viviana, and I don't think you're happy.'

'And this is how you save me?' I showed him my wrists, which were covered in bruises and marks.

I regretted saying that. I shouldn't have confronted him, slaughtered him with logic; it would shatter his fantasy. Davi might get jumpy. Which indeed he did. Elegantly jumpy. He simply walked over to the door and locked it from outside again, taking the key with him. I thought about running after him, stopping him from leaving, but I didn't want to find out what he was capable of in that state. I was beginning to understand how it worked: whatever happened to me, I would get the blame. I would be the one who made him lose his head, and any rational justification I offered would be fuel to the fire.

I took a breath. I thought to myself: you thought you were going to die and you haven't. Yet. You have a shot at escaping. If you focus.

Without making a sound, I peeped out through the keyhole. The living-room light was on and he was reading on the sofa. I thought about calling him, acting docile, seducing him. But playing the girlfriend wouldn't get me anywhere. I was beaten and bruised, the henchman was too close by, they'd already gone and fucking kidnapped me, and if they let me go I might go and tell the world and his aunt. Even if I did escape and reported them, his father

147

would doubtless pay off the police: I was only a woman, and a prostitute to boot, not even a white one. But Davi was afraid of his parents, who were in turn afraid of damage to their reputation. Maybe he didn't realise it, but César was also there to keep an eye on him. I might have become that kind of idiot if I had been super-protected, if I hadn't seen the world in all its splendour and repugnance from early on, I pondered, my hand on my cheek, sitting back down. I had two options: either try to escape or play along until they decided to let me go, feigning compliance and cooperation. Both options carried risks. If I stayed, César could decide that the best thing was to kill me and bury the evidence there and then, so that the family didn't run into difficulties. What would stop him from burying me under one of his boss's numerous cattle pastures? He had turned off my phone the moment he kidnapped me and then taken it away along with my bag. He was already erasing every trace of me, the fucking shithead goon. If I managed to survive another day or two, would I have a chance of being found? Lucinda and Grazi must already be worrying about my disappearance. Josefel would be fine, I knew that Lucinda would look after him if I ended up in a ditch.

Suddenly I heard the key in the lock, then the door creaked open and Davi entered, looking at me slantwise. He locked the door and put the key in his pocket. I remained seated on the toilet lid the whole time. He went over to the sink and removed the heavy old mirror above it. He placed it carefully on the floor. He opened the cupboard below the sink, inspected everything inside and then closed it. He tried to open the cupboard in the corner, no luck, locked. He looked up at the small chandelier; he inspected the bin and took from it the bits of the rope with which César had tied my hands and put them in his pocket. He looked inside the shower door, where there was only an expired shampoo bottle and a dried-up bar of soap in a rusty metal holder hanging from the tap of the electric shower. Davi picked up the holder with the shampoo, conditioner and soap, and left it next to the mirror. He looked at the tilting window up high, without appearing to be bothered by it. Finally, he ran his eyes across the entire bathroom and seemed satisfied.

'Nothing can hurt you now,' he assured me. 'Rest easy.'

Gobsmacked, I watched him leave, taking the mirror and the shampoo holder with him and locking me once more in that freezing room. They looked more like anti-suicide measures to me than precautions to stop me from using any of those items to escape. There was nothing left that I could use to hurt myself with. It was very revealing that he considered this a possibility. In his head I might kill myself out of desperation, for not being able to escape. Or maybe to hurt him, since he already believed I hated him. What was interesting was that he believed I would kill myself because of *him*.

I realised that, essentially, Davi's reasoning was very simple; even the Hamlet of agribusiness had to have his Ophelia. If in his head I was his soulmate, then I had to be a tortured soul, just like him. And I would act in the same way he must have acted at times.

What a massive narcissist.

In the meantime, his impulse to protect me from myself might come in handy. I didn't yet know how, but it would somehow. I remembered a documentary about psychopathic killers that I'd once watched while channel-hopping at home. Psychopaths had one-track minds, obsessed with their goals; there was no use arguing with them, they couldn't be duped, basically you were screwed. But if Davi wasn't one, and I didn't think he was, then what I needed to do was to continually emphasise my humanity. The more human he considered me to be, the better chance I had of getting out of there alive and in one piece, because when a person was robbed of humanity anything was permitted. I needed to avoid him reaching the conclusion that *I can do what I want with that one; no one will care.* In other words, I had to be more than *just a hooker.*

I had a brief discussion with myself – how would I come up with a third persona that wasn't too out of touch with my escort personality nor the idealised image he had of 'my true self'? Neither Vívian, nor Viviana; who would I be now? I was beside myself with rage, which could compromise my ability to do this properly. But I had to survive. What I had to do was use the tricks of my trade – evaluating clients and strategically putting on a persona – to distance myself from the unreal world associated with it. Strike through the heart and come out the other side. Was this madness?

I listened to the crickets outside, the sounds of the countryside that I could not appreciate in such circumstances. I thought about Grazi, the state she must be in, about Lucinda and Mum, how they'd feel if I stayed missing for a long time or turned up dead, and I thought about Josefel. I was cold and hungry, my feet were bare and frozen, and I had a metallic taste in my mouth and an empty stomach churned by stress. I was in a poker game and my hand was weak. The only way out was to bluff, and to bluff well.

'Davi!' I called. 'Davi!'

There was a short delay before I heard some movement. Because of the delay, I figured he had hesitated before coming to me. I heard the key turning in the lock, then the door opened and Davi stood in the doorway like a two of spades, without coming in, looking at me suspiciously. I had my arms crossed over my chest, each hand massaging the opposite arm, and was sitting down to look smaller and more fragile.

'It's very cold,' I said.

He looked at me a moment longer and made up his mind:

'Back in a minute.'

He left the door open. He came back with a big bulky thing all squashed into royal-blue polyester, his hands hooked round it like he was holding a very light tray. A sleeping bag. His thumb was lightly pressing down on the top of the heap to keep its shape: big hands, I noticed, remembering. He came closer and placed it down on the bidet, stopping to my left.

'Thank you.'

He stood there looking at me in silence. He didn't know how to look after people, I thought; he was always the one being looked after, never gave caring any value. He thought people looking after him was the natural order of things, the norm, he didn't understand why that had stopped being the case, why random women didn't automatically attend to him, as his mother used to do, and his nannies, servants and teachers. I hadn't asked for anything, I had only said that I was cold, I had shown weakness and *he* had decided to do this for me. He seemed almost transformed by this unexpected role of carer, of minor saviour. He hadn't known he possessed that capacity, that power.

So, I thought, I need to ask for things. Ask without asking, with a certain reluctance, as if my wounded pride were slowly subsiding, like a fever. Me, victim of circumstances; you, Tarzan. Now I was in my territory. I felt my professional muscles warming up to take on that hooker's job, role play; the closest thing to therapy I was capable of offering.

'So you're going to leave me here until the bruises have gone,' I said. 'Then I can go?'

He nodded quickly and so did I.

'Good. Now I know I'll get out of here I feel calmer.' I smiled. 'I was already planning to change career. I'm tired, you know.'

'I understand,' he said, with an understanding half-smile. 'You weren't happy.'

'Yes, you're right,' I said, feigning mild resistance to having to admit he was right. I got up and began unfolding the sleeping bag. It was obviously imported, one of the best brands on the market. I rolled it out on the floor and thanked him again.

'Thank you.'

'See you tomorrow,' he said.

'See you tomorrow.'

The door closed, then the key turned. I switched off the light and found myself in almost total darkness. Now the only light was what came in through the tilted window. I got into the polyester cocoon and started to zip it closed. My frozen feet were crying out for a pair of socks, but I wasn't going to ask for some – not at that time of night.

Once I was comfortable and warm in the sleeping bag I realised, in my drowsy state, that deep down I wanted to give in. I was finding it almost easier to try my luck being obedient, sleeping there and, in the morning, continuing to play the reformed Magdalen for Davi. My mind, however, was kicking back, refusing to let me fall prey to this temptation, this bait. I argued with myself: you're in the *Arabian Nights*; if you don't tell the sultan a good story, you'll be dead by morning. I've always thought that the sultan can't have loved his women all that much, seeing as he killed them the moment the wedding night was over; he wanted to attain something through them, at the very least not to be a cuckold. My sultan had not even deigned to offer me dinner. Afraid to use his big hands; I would be too weak for them... that was the story he told himself. To tell the truth, he feared losing control over himself and, by extension, over me (that was what I was to him, basically: an extension). He also didn't know if he was capable of caring for me and being responsible for me, as well as for himself and the family farms. He was scared of finding out. That was why he'd chosen me, the hooker... a secure, controllable object. A teddy bear. But now I had to stop being that, or he'd never be able to leave his dependency behind him. It was my obligation to rebel, not to make it too easy for him.

I was justifying a decision which I had already taken to myself. I couldn't believe in my own pretending. Everything was not fine. It would not turn out fine. I couldn't afford the luxury of lying here waiting for him to take pity on me, nothing was guaranteed. I had to believe I was in genuine danger and that the longer I stayed there, the worse things could turn out. I needed to give them the slip. Becoming a damsel worth rescuing was plan B.

Right. If I was going to escape, this was the best time, with the henchman in another house and my official captor asleep. He was asleep, wasn't he? I got out of my sleeping bag and put my ear up against the door, then my eye to the lock. Total darkness. If he wasn't sleeping in the living room he must be somewhere else in the house.

I grabbed the crochet toilet paper holder from inside the sink cupboard and took it over to the light from the window. I examined it all over, trying to find some piece of wire inside that might be useful in my attempt to open the lock. But the crochet on the holder was given its shape by flat hard plastic strips and, on the top, a ring made from the same material. Was the ring too thick to work as a screwdriver? I went over to the locked cupboard and tried it out on the screws on the hinges: yes, too thick. I felt around in the back of my trousers, in search of a coin in my pocket, only to discover there were no pockets. Before cursing all women's clothes, however, I put my hand inside my blouse and unhooked my bra, praying that there would be a metal underwire. But it was a very chic model, with a structure made from plastic. Damn plastic.

Then I felt around the back of my head. I had hairpins. One on each side, holding my quiff in place.

I had learnt to open locks with everyday objects several months before. I was playing an RPG in which breaking locks was one of the skills that improved with experience. I was addicted to it and even installed the game on Grazi's computer in São Paulo, and when I was in her house I'd continue my campaign with the bow-woman Calleigh, whom I'd created after being disappointed with the progress of my first character, the ogre Sheela, and starting again from zero. Calleigh was a covert thief and a crack shot, and her development pleased me to such an extent that reality dulled in comparison.

'It's a shame breaking locks isn't so smooth in real life,' I said one day to Grazi, laughing.

She also laughed and said, with an air of defiance:

'Who said it isn't?' She went up to the computer and pulled me off my chair. 'Want to see?'

It seemed like Graziane had done it throughout her teenage years. That was how she and her friends had had fun in her hometown. That was how they'd found the best places to fuck and smoke or simply not be disturbed. That was how they stole things from locked drawers, like in matinee films.

'Locks on drawers are easier. You can even open them with hairpins.'

'You delinquent…' I teased her.

I watched her with curiosity, as she sprung open lock after lock, using different bits of paraphernalia, from clips to forks. When my turn to try arrived, I found I was terrible at it, and besides I really wanted to go back to my game, which I was good at. I wanted to give up, but she didn't let me.

'What if you pick up a crazy client and he locks you up?'

'Touch wood that never happens.'

That day had arrived. Grazi had made me train until I did it – that day, my hard-won victory made me feel elated – and I would never properly be able to thank her unless I managed to repeat that feat again now, for real. I love you Grazi, I thought. Another thing I could only tell her if I stayed alive.

Using a nail and a tooth, I twisted one of the hairpins to a ninety-degree angle and turned the other one into a straight wire with its tip ending in an L. I pulled the rubber tips off the ends and spat them out. I stuck the first pin into the lock. I felt my way around inside and soon realised that the cogs were very loose; it was an old door with one of those giant locks from a castle's sleeping quarters. My skills as a lock picker didn't add up to much, especially considering these tiny, improvised tools.

But there was another door, I thought, another door with a simpler lock that I could try. Perhaps I'd find something useful that would help me to escape. The small, modern lock on the Formica cupboard, a recent addition to the bathroom, received the pin at a straight angle as if it had been made for it. I applied a bit of force in the same direction as the real key would turn to open. Then, beneath it, I inserted the tip of the L-shaped pin all the way to the back of the mechanism, put my ear up to it and pulled back emphatically. I felt five little clicks in succession, but the top clip didn't turn any further, as should have happened if I'd got it right. OK, it wasn't that easy: as Graziane had taught me, it took calm and patience. And perseverance. It was possible to poke around with the L-shaped pin bolt by bolt while continuing to apply pressure to the top part, which would eventually turn. I pushed the L to the back and started again. My only light source was the glare from outside, and it was so weak I ended up closing my eyes, trying to use my ears to gauge the tiny distances between each bolt, and trying to achieve this with a precision that grew more obsessive by the minute. When I sensed that the upper pin wasn't going to turn I took them both out of the hole and started again from scratch. I tried once, twice, five times; twenty-five, thirty times. That's how I had managed to open the lock the other time, with Grazi: my eyes closed, concentrating on listening to the internal mechanism. If I turned on the bathroom light I might alert César, somewhere outside, or Davi. I felt that I was almost there (forty times); I counted the bolts in the lock, applied pressure as gently as possible (fifty times), but the key wouldn't turn. This wasn't a game, it was a question of life or death; the abacus in my head wanted to explode and lose count, but I wouldn't let it. On the seventieth attempt, the upper pin finally turned.

My tired but grateful hand finally stopped rotating the cylinder. I pulled the double doors back and looked around. In my amazement, it took me a while to acknowledge the prize that was waiting for me inside: cleaning materials. Bleach, broom, brush and a small folding stepladder, which I opened below the folding window without making a sound. There was also a foldable plastic stool, which I balanced on the last rung of the ladder. I calculated that if I stood on it my chest would be at window height, and I could fit my body through and escape. But it was a blind leap and the fall on the other side could be substantial. Besides, I didn't know what awaited me on the other side. Still, I'd try.

I picked up the sleeping bag, climbed the ladder and then stood on the stool. I opened the window as far as it would go, forcing the rusty handle, and looked out: I saw the edge of the roof where it met the eaves and a bright light coming from an unknown location. I threw the sleeping bag towards the outer wall, to cushion my fall. I heard how long it took to hit the ground. Was I really about to do this? It was madness. I squeezed my head and arms through the window. I saw the sleeping bag waiting for me down there, the concrete border surrounding the house, the flat terrain lit up behind it. The gap was big enough for me to get through, but I would have no space to manoeuvre and I'd fall, head first and arms extended. I'd bash myself up a bit, sure, but nothing serious. The craziest thing would be to stay here, I thought, and I drew strength from remembering similar escapades from my childhood and adolescence: jumping ten metres off the trampoline, swimming to the next beach, jumping off a big rock into the water – with zero consequences.

I slid half of my body out until I was almost folded in two, my bum slightly stuck in the gap in the window, my arms, face and chest scraping on the harsh surface of the outside of the house. I could still go back if I wanted, but what I did was protect my head with my arms, close my eyes, stick out my legs and then, just like that, I dived out. One of my shoulders and the side of my body were the first to meet the ground, then my legs, which caused me to slip off the sleeping bag. I felt each shock and bump; my eyes still closed, I straightened my body very slowly, feeling several different pains, mainly in my shoulder. I had a deep graze on one of my arms from hitting the cement as I'd landed. I half-opened my eyes and raised my injured arm, still stunned. Dark blood was seeping from a straight mark along the forearm, and ruby-red dots traced different patterns around it. I kept moving my body slowly, to check if anything else was wrong. I didn't seem that bad. A dazzling light pointing towards the side of the house, perhaps to keep away thieves (cattle thieves?), made me turn my eyes away. I sat down, breathed in, raised my head and then my whole body. I began walking in the direction of what I thought was the front gate. I could only use one arm but my feet were in one piece, and that was what mattered. My plan was to make a discreet exit from the ranch and not stop until I found the main road.

Suddenly, I heard footsteps. I ran without looking back. A loud gunshot whistled as it passed me. I ran even faster, charging towards the house, to get out of the line of fire.

It was the henchman, without a doubt. Another shot, this time trying to hit me before I turned the corner of the house. But I managed to get away in time. Then I tripped on the front steps and fell facing the front door, which opened at the same time, almost frightening me to death. For the first time since it all started I shouted, dragging myself backwards as I sat on the floor.

It was Davi who emerged from the door. Framed like an angel by the illuminated threshold, he looked at me in indignation, as if I was the only one responsible for this annoying problem, this disruption of the order of things. He turned his face to one side. César came walking over with the pistol pointed straight at my head, adjusting the sight. Davi raised his hand to signal 'stop' and said:

'Mate, what's going on?'

César did not obey and kept walking forward with his weapon pointed at me, hoping to finish me off right there. He must have been thinking that once it was done it would be done, problem solved. But Davi placed himself in front of me, breaking the line of fire once again. And I'm certain he saved me.

'She tried to escape,' said César, lowering his gun but keeping it out.

'You're not going to kill her,' David said.

'She won't stay quiet.'

'That doesn't mean you have to kill her, C. Understand?' Davi loomed over him, something which seemed unprecedented, and César's displeasure at this fact was as visible as Davi's pleasure in something which probably didn't happen that often: Davi acting the part of the boss.

'Put that gun away. Let me deal with her. Go away,' he said.

César locked the gun away, shot one last angry look at me and began returning to the cabin house, where the security light must have been installed.

'And you,' Davi said, moving closer to me, 'come here.'

He grabbed me by the wrist of my injured arm and pulled me up from the ground. My shoulder hurt, my forearm hurt, and my eyes stung with pain and frustration. Tears ran down. I thought I was going to escape but instead I'd nearly died. I might have been caught now, but at least I wasn't going to die. Not for now, at least. Davi shook me.

'Look at me. Stop crying. Open your eyes.'

I took a deep breath and decided to obey. He was very, very close. I was trembling.

'You tried to trick me. You don't do that with me. You don't know me.'

'Sorry.'

'What? I didn't hear you.'

'Sorry, Davi.'

Having loomed over his servant, he now wanted to loom over me. To be honest, that might be advantageous, I thought, remaining strategic despite my dire circumstances. Davi held me, and I realised he didn't know how to show me who was in charge. I decided to help him.

'I was scared,' I said. 'You gave me no food or water. I thought you were going to kill me.'

'I'm not going to kill you. But if you escape again, we'll have a problem, because César prefers to resolve things with bullets. And I won't come between you again. You were lucky this time.'

Or rather, *don't think that I like you all that much.* That was my window to say: *Oh, please, like me that much.* I nodded and looked down in humiliation. *My lord, I am not worthy.*

'Here's what we'll do,' he continued. 'You're going to sleep with me. But you need to *actually* sleep. I'm not going to stay up all night watching you. If you need to, take a Rivotril. I've got some.'

'OK,' I said.

And as he took me into the house, I asked him:

'Do you have anything I could line my stomach with first?'

'In the kitchen.' Then he remembered I was his prisoner. 'I'll come with you.'

I followed him into a huge, cold farm kitchen, with tiled mosaics on the floor. It was me who turned on the light; he had headed straight for the fridge, believing its light would be enough. A wall clock read 1:10 a.m.; I think it was correct. I searched for any knives on display but found none, so I went to the fridge with him. Inside there were only onions, butter, water and an open bag of bread rolls. And there I was expecting some farm-fresh eggs, a bit of steak maybe...

'It's pretty empty,' he said, grabbing the rolls and butter. 'César will go shopping tomorrow. He wakes up so early.'

'Wow, he can't sleep much then. How old is he?'

'Forty, forty-five. Why?'

'Older people sleep less?'

I looked discreetly over his head. At the other end of the kitchen, next to the closed back door, there was a decorative casserole hanging from the wall. A potential weapon, I thought, but as well as being out of reach it had no handle, which would make it difficult to hit someone with it. Even so, I took note of its position; it could come in handy later on.

Davi took a bunch of keys from his pocket and tried out several different ones until he managed to open one of the cupboards under the sink. I saw him reach out his hand and take down a pudding plate, and at the back, I identified a wooden knife block, the kind that people usually have out on their kitchen surface. Davi had used a cooking knife to free me from the ropes: it must have been below the sink, now back in its block. From a drawer with no latch Davi pulled out a blunt, flat knife and began cutting the rolls in half and portioning out bits of hard butter.

Those locks were old, they hadn't been installed for my sake. Locks in the kitchen are there so that the servants don't steal food or the silver cutlery, I thought. But there, from the looks of it, they were also used to hide sharp knives. What kind of person would think of taking that kind of measure? Someone who was scared of a violent death in a domestic setting and possessed a morsel of power. Locking away the knives must have been Davi's mother or grandmother's idea, the sort of thing a woman under attack would do in an attempt to avoid the worst: death, scandal. Bruises from beatings vanished within a few days.

This was a house of aggressors, then – if it hadn't been clear to me before it certainly was at that moment.

I noticed Davi's gaze switching between the butter knife in one hand and the roll in the other. He looked indecisive. About what? What was challenging about making bread and butter? He really wasn't right in the head. I pretended I hadn't noticed anything.

It wasn't like in the movies. There was no evil genius. It wasn't a conspiracy. I didn't know too much, and I hadn't stolen any nuclear secrets. And no one had planned a fucking thing. My kidnapping was more like a chapter from *Don Quixote* or some other comedy of errors. It was classic Brazil. No one here has the money or the time or the patience to watch you, bug your car, follow you on the street. Or pay someone competent and trustworthy to do it. The motivations are nebulous, even the perpetrator doesn't really know they're planning a crime: it's a spur of the moment thing. Once they realise they're already committing one, they jump the gun. And the measures taken to avoid problems are half-baked and shoddy too. Always addressing the immediate problem without ever planning ahead.

Davi went back to spreading the hard butter on the bread, but now in a way that was frantic, brutal even. With a certain horror, the thought lodged itself in my head: César and Davi were not in fact a sinister gang, devoted to crime. They had an almost familial relationship and that was what had led them to do this. Davi had confided in César about me and César had decided to act. He'd followed me since my arrival in São Paulo and had suddenly decided to capture me, relying on the lack of security in the city and my potential desire to get with a rich kid, albeit a problematic one, to move up in life. That way, their withered family tree could bear fruit. Family ties, in the sense that the Mafia were also a family.

What César hadn't considered was that I might not view this as a good opportunity and instead try to run away from the charming prince like the devil from a cross; when he realised this he immediately started seeing me as a hindrance, and decided I was better off dead. I didn't want any of that, I didn't want to be saved, I was doing great. If not quite rich, I was doing fine, healthy, in love with someone who understood me and wanted to be with me. Helping my family. I could get out of the game, I had money already invested and more to invest. Even if Davi had offered me a good long-term contract for my company, something he didn't want to do out of pride, I wouldn't have accepted it. Davi had nothing to offer me, not even as a client; it would come to represent a loss of freedom and sanity. It was even more obvious from the inside. As obvious from the inside as it was impossible to understand from the outside. That was always my curse.

I watched Davi hacking away at the bread, demolishing it in the process. Suddenly I had an optimistic thought. They couldn't have known much about me. They couldn't have thoroughly investigated me, or talked about me; it was possible they had different concepts of who I was. Perhaps they didn't know I came from a family of judges and lawyers and that, no matter how many cards Davi's father had up his sleeve, there would be consequences when I was found – no matter what state I was in. Perhaps they didn't know I had a girlfriend and viewed Graziane simply as a close colleague. Perhaps they couldn't even see me in a relationship with a woman or felt that a woman being with another woman didn't count. They didn't know that she'd quickly realise I was missing, that she might have already realised even though it was only the night of the first day, and she'd do anything to find me. As would my sister, and my father, and my mother. They must have assumed I wasn't close to my family. If I was smart, then, and managed to string them along, I could buy enough time for someone to find me.

All signs pointed to Davi being the weak point. He knew I was intelligent but wanted to believe he was more intelligent. He knew I had a personality but wanted to believe that his could also be enthralling. Only as a case study… and there was a reason I'd quit psychology after the second semester.

He gave me a buttered bun. He'd made seven, which was all there was in the bag. We both began to eat.

'What brand is this butter?' I asked, my mouth full.

'None,' he replied, his mouth also full. 'It's local.'

'Really good.'

So far I'd achieved a few things with Davi, including that 'meal', continually driving home that I was a human being who experienced cold and hunger. I wondered if I should try asking for a phone too, claiming that I needed to put my family at ease; perhaps I'd be able to send a coded SOS? But if I asked to speak to my sister or mother, it could go one of two ways: either using one of their mobiles, which they wouldn't want because it would implicate them; or using my own phone, with them writing and sending the message for me, so that they had more control. However, if they gave me back my own phone, they'd have free access to my device, which was the last thing I wanted. They would find out too much about my life and loved ones. It would harm both them and me. Best not to ask for any phones and just hope they found me.

Suddenly I looked at the table to see that there were no rolls left. Davi had eaten them all. I looked at him in shock.

'None left?' I asked.

'Now you can take that pill,' he replied, and pulled me into the living room, leaving me on the sofa.

Davi went into the bedroom and came back with two oval-shaped pills and a stainless-steel jug filled with water. He poured it into a tall, cylindrical glass, downed a pill with some water and said:

'So you know that I'll sleep too.' He pointed to the other pill on the table. 'Take it.'

I looked at the pill and saw that it wasn't Rivotril. I know my drugs. I picked up the small white oval, placed it in my mouth and took a generous draught from the glass of water. I swallowed.

'You think you can trick me,' he said.

Davi grabbed my chin and pressed down on the sides of my face. I started coughing as cover but he invaded my mouth with a metallic, starchy finger. I bit his hand and received a slap that knocked me to the ground. He took advantage of this to get on top of me and rescued the pill from its hiding place right beneath the lower left corner of my tongue. He held my jaw open with two fingers of his other hand and shoved it right into my uvula. Then he covered my mouth and nose with ease.

'Swallow.'

The pill was poking into my throat at the worst possible angle and I managed to suppress the urge to vomit, but I was still so desperate that despite all my different aches and pains, new and old, I shook my body to get free of the hands that were suffocating me. The one thing that was clear was how trapped I was and how much that situation excited him. If Davi wanted to, he could kill me there and then; in fact he was beginning to do just that. I stopped. I gave a thumbs up and tapped the hand over my nose softly, the universal sign that a sex game is over when you can't talk or forget to agree on the signal beforehand. He slowly lessened the pressure on my nose, but at his own pace, as if once more he wanted to show who was in charge. But he kept his hand on my mouth; I was still being punished. The pill was still lodged in my throat and I had to gather all the saliva I could, biting my tongue, which had gone dry from fear, to swallow it. I couldn't stop thinking about my cat, to whom I gave pills in the same way. Never again, I thought. I'll find another method.

Gasping, furious, I looked at him. He made me open my mouth and show him every corner of my tongue. This time a simple order was enough to make me obey.

'Better than dying, huh?' he said.

I couldn't conceal my hatred.

'That wasn't Rivotril,' I said through gritted teeth.

'It's similar.'

'Is that your first of the day?' I asked, knowing it wasn't.

'I'm a big man. I need two.'

I slowly raised myself up from the floor and sat on the rug, my back against the sofa. Sitting next to me he seemed completely relaxed, despite having almost strangled me to death half a minute ago. That made me certain that the sedative we'd swallowed wasn't Rivotril but one which, if you resisted the initial hypnotic effect, gave you a great feeling of peace and then left you completely out of it. Hallucinations and bizarre sleepwalking, as well as assaults on the fridge, reckless driving, compromising phone calls and sex. Then, a delicious amnesia that was often brought up in trials as a mitigating circumstance for all kinds of crime. Davi had taken a pill, resisted sleep, made bread and butter for us (mostly for him) and now he had taken another. Shit. If I'd known beforehand what kind of pill he'd taken I'd have chosen to sit down with him on the sofa for a casual chat instead of risking being attacked by that knife he'd made sandwiches with in the kitchen.

'You know, Viviana, I just thought that there was a much easier way of stopping you escaping. Taking off all your clothes. If you were naked you wouldn't even need to take the medicine, because you'd be unable to escape. We're so dumb, aren't we?' He laughed. 'We didn't even think of that.'

Speak for yourself, pal, I thought. Now, vaguely aware of what I had taken, I thought over my options. I couldn't go to the bathroom and vomit. I couldn't let myself drift off to sleep before Davi, no way, not with him going on about taking off my clothes. I had to fight off sleep, but not to the point of being so high that I tried to escape again, with the henchman waiting to kill me as soon as I set foot outside the house. I had to fight off sleep until Davi was unconscious. Then I'd sleep too, right away. That was my only option. Meanwhile, he insisted on blabbering on endlessly. Remorselessly.

'Viviana, I don't know how you feel about children. Are you planning on having any? How many?'

While I considered how to reply to this random question, he answered for me.

'Because the only thing I make a point of is not having children. No children.'

And yet he hadn't wanted to use a condom for the second round of our encounter months earlier. Of course, I hadn't let him. Besides everything else, it wasn't a relationship. It was madness, nothing made sense and he kept on talking, piling up more and more words on top of me, as I groped around in the dark, looking for the thread of the conversation… feeling my heavy eyelids… not knowing how to reply, but also unable to stop replying, because if I did I'd nod off before him and be raped, or he might get offended and attack me again. I didn't want to be a bore to him or to myself. The bore was a great danger when you were dealing with wannabe sultans. I had to swallow it and keep it to myself – another trick of the trade, I thought, and I found it amusing, and laughed. He thought I'd found what he'd just said funny:

'You're gonna love hanging around with us. I can't stand dumb women any more, the kind that post photos of themselves in bikinis with a quote from the Bible. We're gonna take lots of trips together. Not that kind of trip, haha. Though I am mad keen to try ayahuasca... You been to the Amazon?'

I understood what was happening: Davi also wanted me to fall asleep just before him. And he was better at resisting it than I was. Yet by resisting sleep he was getting higher and making less and less sense. I tried to take the piss out of him in my head, but it wasn't enough to keep me awake. Suddenly I was scared of him thinking he was being completely logical as he hallucinated about, I don't know, me wanting to kill him and how therefore he needed to get to me first. I was getting more and more anxious while I listened to him talking about how the ends justify the means, how we were there in very strange circumstances but one day we would look back and have a good laugh about it all, and by the way had I seen *How I Met Your Mother?* It was a series, he explained.

No, I thought, but I have seen *How I Met Your Motherfucker*.

I think I unintentionally ended up saying what I was thinking out loud, because I remember him questioning me, repeating the sentence I'd said in my head. I don't know if he took it badly or laughed. Then I think sleep won me over, or amnesia wiped everything out, because I only remember fragments. We woke up lying in each other's arms, with César saying 'Morning, lovebirds' as he walked through the living room with several plastic bags towards the kitchen. I almost felt happy to be alive.

Then I lowered my hand down my body and saw that I wasn't wearing knickers. I froze.

'Well, well,' said César, coming straight back. 'This slut really is good for something, huh?'

'Take a hike, César, go on,' said Davi, annoyed, although I detected a hint of pride in his voice.

'The change,' said César, handing Davi a bunch of notes. I'd covered myself up with a cushion, and it was only by doing so that I stopped César from seeing me naked, because he tried to have a peep without even attempting to hide it.

'You sure can be vulgar,' I complained.

'Look who's talking,' he shot back.

'Get out of here,' I said.

'You the boss now?' He raised his eyebrows, softly chuckling. 'Wow, world record.'

Davi told César to be quiet and sent him out, this time in a more serious tone.

'Sorry,' Davi said, turning towards me. 'He's a farmhand. Untamed, you know. But he's got a heart of gold and he's super loyal. It'll take some time for him to get used to you. He'll warm to you eventually.' Davi looked at me in delight.

Was this his way of trying to say that I was joining the family? I ran to the bathroom, shut the door and examined between my legs. I had a flashback of lying on my back, folded over the arm of the sofa, head back, getting head and loving it, and I never liked receiving oral sex. I didn't find any semen inside, only lubrication and guilt: I hadn't managed to resist those ten milligrammes of pure pharmacological oblivion. My trousers had been tossed by the wet shower cubicle, the damp face towel thrown over them; it looked as if I'd used it to dry myself. I didn't remember anything. Maybe I'd taken another pill, or several more, after the first blackout. I'd been raped, and in my sleep-walking state I'd cleaned up all the traces of it by myself. I didn't know where my knickers were, and I wasn't going to look for them. I stayed there holding on to my trousers by the hemline for who knows how long, out of it, until I put one of my feet into one of the leg holes, and then the other. I pulled up the zip, did the button and went in search of coffee.

I found Davi engaged in an arduous activity: grinding the beans in a hand mill, filtering the powder into a Japanese glass dripper and serving the resulting liquid in a small tin cup. I hadn't even been there for twelve hours, but it felt like a lot more.

As soon as the smell of coffee reached me, I came out of my trance a little and began thinking clearly again. First, I felt angry at myself. After blacking out, high as a kite, I'd gone to take a shower instead of looking for the keys to the forbidden drawers, or a phone, a gun, anything. As I waited for Davi to hand me the mug of coffee, it dawned on me: César wasn't just being vulgar; he'd been personally hostile towards me after seeing that Davi and I had fucked. But wasn't that what he wanted? His little boss happy, even if it was with the slut who gave as good as she got? Not by the looks of it. There was something more. César was a complex guy.

Now Davi, he was like an onion: no matter how many layers I peeled off, I just found more of the same. It was impressive. The depth of his superficiality. I burnt my lips with the hot coffee and let out a cry.

'Careful,' he said, annoyed like a caring father, taking

173

the mug from my hand. All according to plan, however, looking out for me. Angel of God, my guardian dear.

I touched my lips and said it wasn't serious. Even so, he made a point of rubbing some balm on my lips. I was baiting him to come out of his passivity by making myself a proud victim. Too proud to ask for help, too stubborn to accept it when it was offered. In doing so I became human in his eyes, and he came away with a heightened sense of self-esteem. By believing that I didn't know what was best for me and deciding for me he felt capable, powerful, a knight of honour. That fit well with his internal narrative about the two of us: that only he knew what I needed (and that included him) – and this 'concrete' confirmation of his ideas must have brought him great pleasure. Whereas if I went and asked for help, even if I clearly needed it, I'd become a drag, and lose my appeal. I had to ask without asking.

What I really wanted to figure out was: why me? Wasn't there a whiter nerdy hooker for him to fall in love with? Was Davi like the guy in a whorehouse who decides to flirt with the barmaid, the receptionist or the ugliest or most detached hooker, or the hard-up queen who cleans the place? Like any guy of his kind he probably thought he deserved a prize for having a soft spot for challenges and anything different from the norm. *I love this woman the way she is.* He wanted the rare figurine, the most diffi-cult piece, the beauty others couldn't see. On top of that he'd give himself a pat on the back, feeling like he was doing her a huge favour… And what a man like that could never understand is that any hooker worth her salt would immediately figure out what kind of guy he was and, if she was competent, also know how to create the illusion of conquest, of a challenge gradually overcome, until the job was done.

It was all this, as well as the desire to show off: to be seen around town with his exotic conquest, display her like a trophy. *Look what I found. No one else has one.*

Our double fuck months ago had been good, I'd been a bit bossy and mysterious, not too tricksy but without making it too easy. I was a good beast. He noticed my vinyls, my games and the big tomes on my shelf, asked some questions and saw from my answers that I did indeed know what I was talking about. I had *content*. I *impressed* him, which was no easy task. I was a rare object, and I was still unattainable after I refused to see him for free. I became irresistible to him.

From a few bits of knowledge, he must have gone and decided he was an expert on me. In his opinion, I deserved to share my life with him. All that remained was for *me* to realise how perfect we were for one another, which would happen sooner or later because I was a *smart* girl. Yes. I'd unwillingly dog-whistled, and this guy had heard it, and now he wanted to be attached to me, walk around with me, live out a fantasy of us being soulmates. But not just our fantasy: there had to be some ten people behind our bed. He saw me as a mixture of Sasha Grey and Mia Khalifa, something to show off to his São Paulo friends and fellow agroboys, to his father and even to César, and to make everyone sick with jealousy at his affirmation of masculinity. Check out this conquest. And check out how magnanimous he was: he didn't even mind my being 'exotic' and a little older. He wanted to marry my difference and the fact that I was from Rio, my accent. We'd be a designer couple, gliding around in our own double-mirrored image.

Tears began running down my face, not for the reason he imagined, but it had the same effect. Davi interpreted my crying as feminine fragility, uncontainable emotion. At last, I was ready to leave that life behind.

'Are you happy?' he asked, squeezing my hand.

I wiped away my tears. Like many women, I had ended up playing host to my rapist, a fearful smile glued to my face. At that moment I wished I'd never so much as looked at a man. I wanted to do away with all of them, more than ever. But first, how would I free myself of this particular man? The word no was beyond the kingdom of the conceivable to him, and it was understandable: in the morning light, Davi really was very good-looking, it had to be admitted. Aside from that, he had a big dick, lots of money and was great in bed. I was the crazy one for not wanting all that.

In a certain way he was like me: imprisoned in his own head, obsessed with coffee and books. And I could even detect some bisexual signals coming from him. But the sum of all those things did not make a person to be with, to live with, to give up working for. Maybe he wouldn't even mind if I kept seeing Grazi… and I'd be rich, I thought. But no. I wasn't interested. It disgusted me. It was also deadly boring.

If his plan was for me to agree to accompany him like a well-behaved girlfriend, enjoying his money, then he was far off the mark. But I acted as if he wasn't, and Davi was enjoying it. And this, strangely, was what appeared to be putting César in a bad mood. My theory now was that César had been wanting to kill me since yesterday. If it was just a question of finishing me off, he could have had done it when he kidnapped me, just taken me out to the forest and buried me there. But he'd gone to the effort of taking me to Davi first. Could it be that he wanted to convince Davi to let him kill me? But why?

It seemed like jealousy. The thought crossed my mind that he might have had some sort of pent-up passion for the boss's son. *Brokeback Mountain* kind of thing. Could it be?

I picked up a juicy apple from the fruit bowl in the middle of the table and began to eat it while I thought this over. No, I couldn't imagine either of them being led by such feelings. Men repress those things as deep as possible. The explanation for César's hostility towards me had to be related to a difference in each man's way of thinking, a deeper difference that was camouflaged by the master-and-servant relationship.

I remembered the *Wild Pumpkin* website. Leo and Walter always stood so far apart during recording! Leo right next to me, Walter further away. After I exposed the site for racism, even though they'd been fighting, the two united to defend themselves. I became a rival, and that brought them together. Against me.

That memory helped me understand what could be behind the current situation. César's off-the-record plan was different from Davi's. César didn't want me to be Davi's reluctant girlfriend; he wanted me to fight back to justify the violence he was going to enact upon me. And he wanted Davi to take part. He wanted him to learn *how you treat a woman.*

I understood that I wasn't all that special in this whole mess. It wasn't about me. Any woman could have been swallowed up into that problem, in an attempt to solve it. But from my perspective it *was* about me because it was my body that was there, against my will, intervening in other people's business. I was the altar and the sacrifice.

My anger grew. I chewed my apple in time with my hatred, the fruit and my jaw both crackling. Even my own kidnapping wasn't about me. Thus far I was just an object. And I wasn't even being paid! Sure, no relationship is ever only about the other person, but this was going too far. No one here wanted to use their own body to solve their problems. Without even needing to give an order, Davi had made César, who lived to carry out his wishes and protect him from reality, abduct me. Davi's dependency on others caused him problems, so many that he hadn't even been able to ask those he depended on to satisfy his desire to have me close, so that he could verify if I really was his partner for life, or at least for that phase of his life. César, in part, represented the interests of the family, which viewed a wife as a potential replacement for all that painful self-reflection Davi had to go through in order to get somewhere in life. This miracle wife would shake him out of his inertia and help him realise his limitless potential. If I played along with this little charade, I'd function as a means of restraint for the problematic 'boy', a therapist in the form of a woman. An unpaid psychologist, because paying to talk to one, now that would be undignified.

It just so happens that I could never fulfil the function of a wife where his family was concerned. Not only was I a prostitute, I was also too rebellious, and mestizo to boot. I was meant to serve as a lesson: look what happens when you go after volatile women with an open heart. They rebel against your affections, instead of saying amen. They don't acknowledge your love because they're bad by nature. I was disposable: getting rid of me wouldn't cause too much trouble to such a powerful family. Davi would be complicit in César killing me and he'd understand once and for all how a wife should be: sweet and unremarkable. *You don't take that kind of woman home with you. Have her on the street; your docile wife will pretend she doesn't know.*

It was horrible to think like that. I was trembling and drank a glass of water slowly to hide it. I had come there to die and to turn that boy into a man, in the worst sense. It wasn't just César who had his own plan within a plan, I thought: perhaps the father was also in on my kidnapping, watching it all from a distance. If I feigned sweetness and love at second sight for Davi, it wouldn't give César a motive to kill me and I'd have a chance to hold it together until I was rescued. I had to hedge my bets on that thought.

I started up a conversation with Davi, wanting to show interest in his personality. It was difficult, because the things I asked tended to put him on the defensive, but I managed to extract from him that he hated rodeos and cattle auctions and that kind of thing. He liked animals and so didn't want them to suffer, or rather, in his words, wanted them to suffer 'as little as possible'. He had had his first dog on that ranch. He was a member of the Jockey Club, liked to bet on derbies and had an all-black horse called Beltenebros, but that had been more of an adolescent interest, one which was now fading. Deep down, he confessed, laughing, he always hated that smell of shit. Now he was trying to establish himself as a producer of speciality coffee, starting with some small sample crops. His first plants would soon start production on this very ranch, which had belonged to his grandparents. Though I had never planted coffee, I began to talk to him about my own plants. I told him that I had a big balcony full of them and a little greenhouse with *sinsemilla* in the utility room that I was learning to cultivate, hoping that he had something to teach me and would thus once again feel connected to me – and at the same time, superior to me. But I quickly realised he hadn't the slightest knowledge of agriculture or gardening. I put two and two together: César, who lived on the ranch, took care of everything. At most, Davi would choose the kind of coffee to suit the region's climate and altitude and leave the seeds and the growing to César. Then he'd supervise his employees from afar, hands on hips, while they dug the young plants into the soil. Daddy would pay for everything, including the apartment in São Paulo he'd return to afterwards.

I decided to bring up a topic he'd definitely have something to say about.

'What's your business plan?'

Completely unsurprisingly, the floodgates opened this time. While I paid attention to half of what he was saying, I pondered the new image of the pair that came to me. César and Davi were like lichen on a tree trunk: organisms working together, in symbiosis. The algae and the fungi. One was the active partner in the relationship, protecting it from external threats and consuming sugar; the other, passive partner, was a dependent organism, but one which provided the food for both – through photosynthesis, meaning it didn't have to move. Nevertheless, through its relationship with the algae the fungus could achieve more. It lived longer and better. It was strange how botanists to this day had still not been able to state clearly which was the master and which was the slave in that relationship. Or if those roles even existed.

I realised that I could only survive by clinging to Davi. No asking for a tour of the house or the ranch, no more asking about his family, as I'd planned. Nothing to stir him up. I had to be the lichen's lichen. If I caused too much agitation, the henchman would have the perfect excuse to consider me a threat and eliminate me. That was what all our interactions thus far indicated. Every time I did something active I was attacked. I needed to mimic. I was going to be Davi's rib.

There was no TV and although there was a radio I predicted that any station I could pick up there would not be to my taste. The lights of a brand-new router were blinking below a small table and that was where Davi got his internet from. There were no magazines or newspapers either.

There was a rustic shelf full of books: classics, science and business. As they demanded time and quiet, books always ended up gravitating towards the country house of any family lucky enough to own one, and this was no exception. I walked over to the shelf and inspected it carefully. I chose *Netochka Nezvanova*, an unfinished Dostoyevsky epic which I owned but had never read. I dusted it down with my hand and sat next to Davi, who was already reading. He noted my choice.

'I've read that one, it's really good.'

He was reading a deluxe edition of the *Odyssey*, in a new English translation. The translation was by a woman, not that he told me; I found out by reading the cover. Not that he wasn't dying with pride over his choice, only that it would have been bad taste to rub it in my face, and he had spent his whole life training himself to refrain from shameless self-promotion. Condescending praise for *my* good taste, however, was completely fine; I was meant to feel flattered.

It seemed like the day would pass with no phones, no media, no sound. Davi barely checked his phone and had told me that he wasn't on any social networks, that he found them silly; I could kiss goodbye to the hope he might post something that would bring someone to me. He'd check out for a while and hope that his friends would notice his absence, like it was 1992. Well, not quite, because he was in a WhatsApp group which, he proudly announced, he 'barely looked at' (he'd looked at it over his coffee). Davi, it must be said, could really read: he was capable of a rare level of concentration. But this did not save him, because it wasn't good for him to read that kind of thing. Some people can't deal with fiction, no matter the form.

I was both intrigued and revolted by his lack of self-knowledge, for it allowed him total freedom of action, without any self-questioning. He was free to be horrible. He lived alone with his thoughts, enjoying works of literature and still not knowing himself. I read to escape being swallowed up by my mind, which always ended up going against me, making me know myself better every time as well as understand other people and human relationships. Davi, meanwhile, read so that he didn't have to think about himself, to avoid returning to his own life. He cruised over the surfaces of things, including me. Some people were like that. I remember a university professor saying that the people who'd inspired Chekhov to write *The Cherry Orchard* attended the first night and none of them recognised themselves onstage. Afterwards they even went to congratulate the author. It was that kind of thing.

It was pretty difficult for me to read with the anger and the pain I was feeling, not to mention sitting down, always in the same position. I looked at the new shades of purple that decorated my shins, complementing the scratches and bruises from the abduction. Passing my right hand over my aching shoulder and neck, I felt how hard and swollen they were and, slowly lifting my left arm, saw on its lower part the web of scratches from my frustrated escape attempt. By some miracle, even with all the tugging, the gut punch and the falls from different heights and angles, I hadn't broken anything: maybe it really did pay off to eat yoghurt every day. There might be a sprain or a fracture, but at least it wasn't causing me any trouble, and I was still alive.

Just like when I was a child, I played at understanding the passage of time, judging the sun's progress by the minute, slow movements of the square of light that came in through the window. Now reduced to the bare minimum, the pilot flame, I could survive like a plant during the winter freeze. I could block out my emotions, pretend that nothing was happening to me, that I could stay sitting there, reading next to an androgynously beautiful boy in a pastoral environment, maybe even become his fair maid. The goal was to become fully detached from myself, and I was achieving it. I leafed through *Netochka Nezvanova*, only taking in bits here and there, but when I did manage to pay attention, I saw myself in it, in that difficult childhood in the Russian interior, becoming a servant while still a girl, having no say in the matter. It wasn't my problem, but I turned it into mine and in doing that I untangled myself from me. I turned the page. I looked at Davi. I breathed in and out. I was still alive.

Davi was hungry and made me go into the kitchen with him; then he carried two tuna sandwiches and four napkins over to the table. I chewed the first piece of bread with tuna paste and light mayonnaise my captor had made for me and I remembered those words from *The Little Prince*: 'You are responsible for what you have tamed.' And I had been captured and tamed, like a little animal. He had to look after me. If I were let back into the wild, would I be able to care for myself any more? I remembered to thank him for the lunch, he'd be offended if I didn't.

'Thank you.'

'No problem, Vivi.'

After lunch we went back to the living room. He served himself a single malt with two ice cubes and drank it meditatively from a glass tumbler. He had offered me one too, but I'd said no. I regretted it then: the drink might have numbed the pains I was feeling all over my body. Then I thought that offering me a whisky might have been a test, that he didn't want me to accept such a strong spirit, because he wouldn't want to live with a woman who was a drunk or addicted to prescription drugs. Only he could have vices, it was his prerogative.

He not only expected that we'd be together but that we'd *live* together. Would we manage to get through a whole day of domestic cohabitation? Would I rebel again? He was setting down a challenge. I thought about that house with its locked-away knives and imagined his grandmother sitting in the living room, cancelling some social engagements on the telephone so as not to reveal the marks on her face from the beating she'd taken, and a little Davi realising, little by little, why Granny hadn't gone out horse riding on her own that day, even though she liked it so much. Or his own mother, wearing dark glasses, arriving in a hurry from the capital with little Davi and the driver, to stay at the ranch until the swelling on her face had gone down. First you take the beating, then you take measures to hide it. With time you might find some secret vice to console yourself with. And your son or grandson would soon figure out how it worked.

I imagined Davi wanted to do the same with me, keep me and then let me go, like a strategic commodity. Maybe the idea had come from his own story, his own family's story. But there was no way that this family would let me play such a role. I agreed; I just didn't want to die for it.

Sometimes I caught him admiring me over his book in my peripheral vision, as if he was evaluating me, examining my beauty down to the smallest details, to convince himself that all the trouble had been worth it, that he wasn't wrong, that this woman really was beautiful, inside and out, that she would be redeemed, that her presence would bring him comfort rather than intimidate him. So far, I was passing the test. Not even my scratches, bruises and lack of make-up could break the spell; perhaps he even felt a certain nostalgia for the worn-down women of his family, and – who knows – perhaps even thought he had finally found a suitable candidate for marriage. Thinking this way sent shivers down my spine, and yet I couldn't keep these thoughts away, and was diving ever deeper into them.

The first time we fucked, I'd been turned on, orgasmed, and on top of that charged him extra. But if I'd expected anything else I'd have been greatly disappointed. At first sight, Davi's sunny appearance seemed to promise bourgeois, albeit semirural happiness: horse rides through the countryside, all kinds of luxury, trips to Europe, designer handbags. After sleeping with him a more naïve bitch could, in turn, fantasise about endless bohemias, from nightclubs to yachts, fun *ad infinitum*. But this prince was more like Count Dracula, and he didn't like to leave the house or his own head, where he was king. Not even to sunbathe. In any case, none of that would have interested me.

At around three in the afternoon, when he went to serve himself another measure, I accepted a drink too, though I opted for a bourbon. I accompanied him to the kitchen and watched him take a little bunch of keys from his pocket, unlock the pantry, which was as big as a closet, and open a bottle just for me. While we drank at the kitchen table and talked about the books we were reading, from the corner of my eye I saw a head spying on us through the window. I froze and shouted. Davi's eyes shot to the window, but he saw no one.

'I saw a head there,' I said.

'It must have been César.'

And so it was. César turned, entered the house through the living room and came to talk to us.

'All good in here?' he asked Davi.

'Great,' Davi replied.

César shot me an unfriendly glance, took leave of Davi with a nod and left. He must have been circling the house the whole time, I thought. We're not alone. We have never been alone.

Davi made it clear that it was time for us to go back to the living room. I almost had difficulty obeying. After the bourbon and the shock of seeing César, I was a lifeless, bloodless dead weight. Now I knew that every time César showed his face it would be to try to kill me, if he found an opportunity. Back in the room I dispelled that lethargy, convinced that I had poured away the trauma. Time to act, I thought.

And as if I were only waiting for my own authorisation to proceed, my eyes suddenly focussed on an entirely white spine at the base of the bookshelf. White, curved and tall, taking up the entire space between each pine plank. I got up and went over to the shelf, pretending to inspect the titles until I came to that distinctly bound volume, and took it out to see. Davi stared at me with curiosity. Like someone not searching for anything in particular, I opened the plastic cover, decorated with flowers and with the words MY FAMILY printed on it, and started turning the thick pages inside that photo album – copyright 1983 – by Marsina G. Santos Rodrigues, as the first page announced.

'Did you know about this album?' I asked, sitting down next to Davi.

'I didn't even remember it existed. It must have been my grandmother's.'

Photos of crops, of roots, tangerines and coffee, were a constant. The fruit of the soil. Babies too: children ordered by size, cousins on the porch, the servants' off-spring already helping with cooking and harvesting. In places Marsina had left notes behind the photos, in frilly handwriting. From time to time Davi would let out a comment. *Look at Cousin Genaro, so young. Baby Carol, my God, I can't believe it. What's with that hair, Berê! Wow, my grandad was still alive, I miss him, he was pretty distant, but he loved me. Look at Mum. Look at me.*

'What a little cherub,' I said.

'Little devil, more like,' he corrected.

His mother, as I had imagined, was blonde, and had wavy highlights in her hair à la Farrah Fawcett, which was replaced a few photos later by a perm. On the rare occasions the grandfather did appear he was almost always depicted reading a paper, with his hair all gelled back and glowering, with a very put together Marsina by his side, baring all her teeth. While Davi got carried away by his own memories, I focussed on the photos of the family's servants. A black, middle-aged woman, her greying hair always underneath a cloth, was in several photos, sometimes with children around her. She must have done the cleaning and cooking. In one photo, posing next to a washbasin and a clothes line, she appeared with some other children: *Tetê with her children – 1987*, Marsina had written on the back of the photo. They were all big by then, save one boy who was shorter and lighter than his older siblings. A late-born child, perhaps, conceived with a different person, a lighter-skinned man, I thought.

'Is that César?' I asked, pointing at the child.

'It is! My God, I have to show him.'

In exchange for the crumbs of acceptance he tossed César from time to time, Davi believed that the servant was his friend. As for me... Well, now I was considering the possibility that César was Davi's father's illegitimate son, a foolish act committed as a teenager that he had probably been too scared to tell his own father about – Davi's 'distant' grandfather. And that was why César had stayed. But how must he feel? Did he secretly loathe the false firstborn? Enough to want to kill him? Eliminate the competition? The lichen could cling on to the family tree, but it couldn't kill it, as it depended on it for sustenance. But here the metaphor fell apart, because if that were true then the lichen *was* the tree and it could very easily sprout other branches and continue to subsist. In other words, if he wanted to, César could take a DNA test.

I said nothing. Davi asked me why I'd gone quiet, what I was thinking about.

'My sister,' I replied. 'She was looking after my house and must have returned there today. She might get worried if she doesn't hear from me.'

'Why didn't you say earlier? We'll sort it out.'

We decided to use his phone to send a message to the number I dictated: 'Hey, Lucy, it's Vivi. I'm at a friend's ranch, and there isn't much signal here. Back on Monday. Can you feed Josefel until then please? Xx, Vivi.' We agreed that if she replied Davi would 'have no signal' and leave it hanging in the void. She didn't respond straight away, or perhaps the signal really was bad, but eventually Davi felt a rumble in his pocket and showed me the answer: 'Got it xx'.

I put the album back on the shelf just a moment ago. I reopened the book where I'd paused, and so did Davi. But I'm not reading any more, to tell the truth. I realise it must have been almost twenty-four hours since I was kidnapped. Are they looking for me? Since when? I go over everything I've experienced, everything that went through my head, everything that I did, everything that was done to my body, as the sun sinks lower and lower, projecting oblong forms into the room. Davi doesn't invite me to go anywhere, not to go and see the coffee plants, or get some fresh air, or watch the sunset, not even for a tour of the house. I must make the effort to adapt to him – me, his supposed soulmate. But I already know how things work here. I can't complain. I took my chances and I paid for them; I'm doing the best I can in the circumstances. I'm fed and hydrated and I've convinced him, however incompletely, that I am a human being, an educated woman worthy of redemption. Now I must follow my plan of action, or rather, inaction. Davi thinks everything is fine. César is still looking for an excuse to kill me, because I am a problem and Davi must learn this. I'm not exactly thrilled with the idea of dying, even less dying here, like this, but I understand how things work, and if César continues to be unsuccessful in imposing his will and nothing goes wrong, I might get home alive.

The room starts turning pink: the sun approaching the horizon. My first day as a captive coming to an end. I go back to reading, thinking that there's not long until the end of *Netochka* but – I reflect – as it's an unfinished novel, I'll never reach the end. The light goes through the spectrum and Davi turns on a lamp. When the furniture and walls begin to take on tones of ruby red, earth and, finally, purple, Davi gets up to turn on the main light.

When he returns to the two-seater sofa, Davi looks at me. He waits until I look back at him, and when I look, he sinks his hand into the sofa and exclaims:

'Ta-daa…'

And with his fingers together like a pincer, he pulls some violet knickers out from the cushions – the same ones I was wearing yesterday. He laughs. Though I don't find it funny, I smile. He moves over to me – my torso seizes up, with a pang of pain – and hands me the thong, which I grab from him. He looks at me like he's about to ask 'what?' but he says nothing. I force myself to appear calm, though I'm blinking more than I'd like to. There's something in his eyes. I know what they are saying, but I can't let myself wince.

PART III

JUSTICE

9

LUCINDA

Bit by bit, Graziane manages to stop crying and explains:

'Vivi sent the message from a client's mobile. As if it was to you, but to my number, signalling that she's in danger, not allowed to communicate freely. Understand? I need you to look at her contacts and tell me whose number it is.'

Lucinda goes to the car and sits in the passenger seat with the laptop on her legs.

'Found it. "Davi Agroboy." No surname. But…'

'I know who that is,' Graziane says. 'Rancher's son. His father's an old client of mine. She must be at their ranch.'

'Do you know where it is?'

'Yep. I've been a few times, my phone will remember the location.'

'Grazi… let's tell the police.'

'No. There's no time. She's alive now, but who knows how much longer. This guy's keeping her there, his father's very important. The police will be in on it.'

'What are you going to do?' Lucinda's heart is racing. 'Go there?'

'Don't you understand? No one will do a fucking thing, Lucinda. We have to do it ourselves.'

'Where is this ranch?' Lucinda asks, still unable to believe what they are planning.

'São Paulo–Minas border, Minas side. Two hours by car.'

'Fuck! Shit!'

'I have a stun gun,' Graziane says. 'And a few other bits and pieces. I can meet you on the road and we'll head there.'

'I can't believe what we're doing.'

Lucinda still doesn't believe this, but regardless she arranges to meet Graziane at a petrol station in Fernão Dias, which is on the way to the ranch, and twenty minutes later Graziane emerges from a taxi.

The first thing Lucinda notices is that, in the flesh, Graziane looks like a normal girl. A little taller than average, pretty, nails done up, but normal. T-shirt and jeans. She doesn't have the mythical 'hooker face'. Obviously, this is intentional but… even so Lucinda can't help being taken aback.

'I've shared the address with you,' Graziane informs her as she fastens her seat belt.

Lucinda opens the link and checks it: the middle of nowhere. She is keenly aware that she may well be embarking on a suicide mission.

'You've been to this place, then,' Lucinda asks. 'Any dogs there, a caretaker?'

'There's one guy who does everything: driver, caretaker, rancher. No dogs. At least, not when I was there.'

Lucinda nods and sets off. Two hours, eight minutes' journey, the GPS promises. She aims to get there faster than that. The sun's going down.

'It'll be dark by the time we get there,' she says soon after. 'Best to stop the car at the gate, walk up to the house and scope it out before doing anything.'

'Yeah, that's what I was thinking,' Graziane says. 'As far as I can remember the house isn't right by the gate, there's a driveway.'

Lucinda shakes her head, gripping the steering wheel:

'I can't believe what we're doing. This is madness.'

Graziane says nothing, allowing her to let it out.

'We're going to die, you know,' Lucinda continues.

'We have the benefit of surprise,' Graziane replies. 'And we need to risk it, because the other option is to leave Vivi to die alone.'

Graziane's fixed stare burns into Lucinda's face. In silence, she continues to look straight ahead and drive. Within moments, tears fall down her face and she goes into a fit of sniffing and blinking. But then she wipes them away. She asks Grazi to pass her a tissue from her bag. She blows her nose. She puts her foot on the pedal.

From then on, Lucinda is entirely focussed on the driving and doesn't say a word to Graziane, almost as if she's annoyed with her for showing her such a clear route to courage. Sure, Lucinda had resolved to investigate her sister's disappearance, but beyond a certain level of danger she would have preferred to let others solve it. But no. Grazi has hounded her with a plan that cannot be refuted, blinded by the love she felt for Vivi: if you don't follow suit, it's because you love her less than I do.

What a way to get to know your sister-in-law.

Lucinda goes over martial arts moves in her head, both offensive and defensive. She needs to get in his face, or their faces, from close up, preferably by surprise. She breaks the silence to explain this to Grazi: she must attack first with the stun gun, especially if the guy is armed, and then Lucinda can immobilise and disarm him. If she's unsuccessful, they're both screwed.

'So this guy, the ranch handyman: did you get a good look at him? Is he tall, strong?'

'He's shorter than me, don't know how strong he is.'

Lucinda is remembering the size 39 footprints by the side of the road.

'And this Davi, is he tall?'

'I don't know him personally. But wait.' Graziane quickly puts his full name into her browser and finds some photos. 'He's young. Tall, strongish, not jujitsu strong though.'

Lucinda pieces together the story in her head:

'So it was the driver who kidnapped Vivi. Davi calls the shots. Did you see the video I sent? The footprints of the guy who took Vivi are the same size as my feet. Meaning, it was the short one. If we're lucky it'll just be the two of them.'

What Lucinda doesn't say – and doesn't need to, because Graziane's thinking the same thing – is: *if we're lucky, she'll still be alive.*

10

VIVIANA

Up until now Davi's hand has only passed over me for a brief caress, and for the slap when I resisted the pill, but now... he wants sex again. This time, I'm fully awake, caught unawares, and I don't know how I'll get away.

He puts his book down. He touches my arm and gives me a passionate look, hoping that I also feel his urge. Instead, I realise I'm going to panic. As I try to suppress it, my mind reels, picking everything apart in search of a way out.

How did I not foresee this? Ah, I stuck too firmly to my vision of him as a fundamentally passive guy. I forgot about his narcissistic side, his sense of entitlement: if he wants it then I must also want it, clearly, and so all he needs to do is to show he wants it, which is his passive side working again, the side that doesn't even bother with the work of hunting females. Handsome guys like him who have it all made have never had to devote any time to the art of conquest, they've never had to appear interested or chase you – women just throw themselves in their direction – so they lack any skill or subtlety when it comes to seduction. They might be good at fucking, because that can be inbuilt or come with practice, and anyone who fits that profile will have more than enough opportunities to practise. They end up having almost everything and wanting what little they can't have at any price, because what they're thinking is: I can pay. The world isn't fair.

What's also not fair is how no one can say *no* to these guys, who are so used to paying for any woman or any object they want. What if I say no? A definitive no, 'no more', 'never again': you threw it all away when you kidnapped me, attacked me, raped me, there's no point denying it, I know because I was there, doped up but there, and even before that I only wanted you for money and pleasure, never for company. I was there the whole time. I am my own witness, in person. Even so, I fell into the magical thinking of not believing it could happen again. Now I must feign acquiescence and I'm not ready for that.

If I do decide to do this and deny what he wants, I will be obliged to say why, and for Davi there will only be one way to extinguish the shame of being accused of kidnap and rape: let César disappear with me. Rewrite the story, with one line erased. But none of that is necessary, I just need to let him, he won't be violent if I let him. So I put the book down and I look at him. He kisses me passionately and intensely, and if this was a film it would be the part when the music soars and I happily surrender to the millionaire. In reality, the only thing that surrenders is my mind. It's folding up like origami, smaller and smaller each time, and smaller, until it disappears. Maybe it's safe in another dimension, like in a B-movie. I think about everything that super-compressed air can do. I think about vacuum-sealed videos, black holes. At least silence is allowed, I think dejectedly. I won't make a sound. He puts his hand inside my blouse. Suddenly, I jolt: someone breaks the silence with a gloomy 'Good evening'.

Davi gets up from me, pissed off, looking over my head and asking, 'What is it?'

It's César, who takes him to one side and whispers something into his ear. I hear Davi ask him 'Are you sure?' Then he looks at me.

'Viviana,' Davi says, 'you only have one sister, right?'

'Just one,' César replies. 'The one who posted this here.'

Davi grabs the phone César holds out to him. They don't show me what's written, but I presume it's a post about my disappearance. César comes over to me with his hand behind his waist, pulling out a weapon.

'Are you going to do it or am I?' he asks, looking at Davi.

'I already said, C, put that shit away.'

'Mr Rodrigues is going to… You, stay put!' says César, pointing a finger at me instead of a gun. I stop trying to edge away. 'Mr Rodrigues is going to have a fit. He's got heart problems, do you want to kill him, Davi? Fuck's sake. You made me grab this slut off the street, bring her—'

'Shut your mouth!' I shout, taking a shove from César as a result. Davi holds his arm back.

'Shut your mouth!' César shouts, trying to come at me. Davi holds him back.

'Calm it, César. She's already sent her sister a message. She's OK now, she'll delete the post.'

'What?' César wriggles free of Davi. 'You sent a message?'

'On my phone. I lent it to her.'

César takes a deep breath, strokes his chin. He's holding himself back, so as not to react, so as not to call the boy king a fool.

'I typed the message,' Davi explains, agitated. 'I said she's at a friend's ranch and there's no signal there. It's all good, César. Her sister will delete the post, on Monday she goes home, everything's back to normal.'

César shakes his head.

'You're still young, Davi, you have a lot to learn. This woman's playing you.'

'But if she goes home without a scratch, what's the problem?'

'You can tell from looking at her that she won't stay quiet. How's she gonna keep her mouth shut out there if she won't even keep it shut here?'

This time, it's Davi whose mouth stays shut. César continues:

'Don't you realise you've created proof that she's here? As well as getting you into trouble it could harm your family.'

Davi stays quiet. He shoots a glance at me, then at the floor.

'But there's still a way,' César says. 'If your phone is the only proof, we make it disappear and say it was stolen, hacked, any old shit. I turned her phone off the moment I caught her on the road, and I haven't turned it back on. I checked there was no security camera nearby, we weren't filmed. You haven't exchanged messages recently, have you?' César places his left hand on Davi's shoulder and looks him in the eye. 'Step outside, give me fifteen minutes, I'll take care of everything.'

For a moment it looks like Davi has given in, but only for a moment.

'Enough, César. Fuck's sake!'

Davi places himself between us again. César has the pistol in his hand again, ready to shoot at any moment. At the end of the day, once the wrong has already been done, it's best to get on with it. Brandishing his weapon behind his body César gestures towards me with his head.

'What did you see in this woman, kid? She's not even hot. Ugly bitch, big nose. You're going to swap your family for that? You'll ruin your dad. Take a walk outside…'

César walks as he talks, searching for new angles to target me with the greatest precision. I feel defeat is near. I have to save myself. I need to snap out of it and say something in my favour.

'Davi, I could be pregnant.'

The two of them look at me at the same time. César is the first to react.

'From your pimp?'

'From Davi. We didn't use a condom yesterday, and it's one of my fertile days.'

'The nerve of this one…' César laughed. 'She's not pregnant. Ain't nothing in there.'

'You were just going on about family,' I say, touching my belly. 'What if this is family?'

'It's a trick. Any one of a hundred guys could be the father.'

'You going to let him talk like that, Davi?'

'Enough,' César says. 'It hasn't even been one day. There's nothing in there yet.'

'What if there is?' I turn towards Davi. 'Then it's your child.'

'It'll come out just as ugly as you,' César says. Then, to Davi: 'I'll be doing you a favour.'

'Give me that,' says Davi, moving towards the gun.

'When he comes out he'll be your boss,' I say.

César raises the weapon towards me. Reflexively, I huddle up into a ball, but there's nothing I can do: he shoots.

11

LUCINDA

Lucinda repeats one last time: you use the stun gun first if you see anyone who isn't Viviana. Even if you miss, I'll jump on them and immobilise them. Graziane nods. Then they get out of the car.

A bright light illuminates the exterior of a farmhouse, five hundred metres away. That's where the lights are coming from; that's where they're going. A caretaker's hut just at the foot of the spotlight becomes visible when the two start going up the path, lighting the way with Grazi's phone torch.

Lucinda realises how her current need to blend in with the shadows contrasts with her lifelong aspiration to be seen. And that Viviana's struggle had always been the opposite – to be able to disappear at will, or at the very least go unnoticed instead of drawing attention. Whenever they played games, growing up, Lucinda would pick the flashy characters, the ones who liked to make a splash or required a fanfare; Vivi had always preferred the stealthy ones, who could sneak in or out, hide from view, and go off the grid without a trace: spies, vampires and rogues. But this time she hadn't disappeared on her terms – not at all. To her, it must have felt like the ultimate betrayal.

Lucinda worries. Maybe Viviana's mind has broken down after all that she must've been through; maybe she panicked, did something she shouldn't, and her body has paid the price. Or maybe, knowing her sister, she's kept up the pretence all the way through and confounded the hell out of those fuckers. That's when they hear the gunshot.

Adrenaline takes over. They run to the house; a few metres away, they see the door on the latch. Lucinda signals for them to go up onto the porch by the window, which has curtains. Graziane pushes her face up to the glass just in time to see a mass of feminine hair jumping behind the sofa and witnesses the scene that Vivi cannot see: César and Davi fighting for the gun and shouting at each other to let go; it's desperate, but Grazi must not and cannot make Vivi aware of her presence. Lucinda tiptoes towards the half-open door and waves at Grazi to get her gun ready. César and Davi fall to the floor with a thump. Lucinda is wondering whether to widen the crack in the door to get a better look when everyone hears the second shot.

This time it's hit someone for sure. The sound was different, more muffled.

'Fuck,' a man's voice cries out.

Before anyone else can react, the door flies open and Viviana runs out, frantic and barefoot. She would have kicked Lucinda in the face if she hadn't got out of the way of the door when she heard the stampede.

César runs out to the porch and remains there, lining up the shot on Viviana. But Grazi acts first.

The gun's wires fly through the air and he falls to one side, convulsing. Lucinda takes his arms and stamps on his hand, which had already loosened its grip on the weapon. But it's impossible, she needs to grab the barrel to disarm him properly.

'Don't touch the gun, Grazi. Kick it away.'

All those hours spent watching cop shows turned out to be good for something.

Lucinda is being given the handcuffs by Graziane when Vivi starts walking back, slowly, in shock. Grazi runs to her, hugs her, while Lucinda finishes adjusting the cuffs tight around César's hands, tied behind his back. He flounders and lets out an endless tirade of whores, sluts, bitches and slags. For the time being, they ignore him.

'What about Davi?' Lucinda asks.

'I'll go and see. Stay here, Vivi.'

Graziane prepares the stun gun for another shot, enters and comes straight back out.

'He's unconscious,' Grazi says. 'The bullet hit him in the stomach. It's a fucking bloodbath.'

'And this one here?'

'Give me the other things, Grazi.'

Protesting and trying to bite, César is silenced with a gag ball. A black rope is tied tightly around his ankles. They enter: Davi's in dire straits, no one wants to go near him. They go over to the opposite site of the porch from César to discuss.

'Shall we call the police now?' Lucinda wants to know.

'Police, ambulance, yeah.'

What they don't verbalise, and don't need to at this stage, is the possibility of simply finishing César off and then leaving. It's not that they don't want to. But not involving the police could be worse; Viviana wouldn't receive the assistance she needs, and if they found proof of her presence, she could be locked away for crimes she didn't commit. Besides, that is a risk for all of them, for being there. And killing someone in cold blood, no matter how much they deserve it, is not a decision that has no moral or mental consequences. Lucinda knows that from everything that has happened so far, she has already banked her fair share of nightmares for the next few years.

EPILOGUE

The two cops from the vehicle that parks right outside the house find us seated on the porch, the gun still on the floor and, a good distance away from us, César, handcuffed, gagged and with his feet tied. Inside, Davi.

When the first shot echoed in the room, I barely had time to huddle up in a ball on the sofa. Only after did I see that it hadn't touched me. Davi had knocked away César's arm and was fighting with him for the gun, each one shouting orders at the other. I certainly wasn't going to interfere. I jumped behind the sofa and wondered if I could run to the door when they fell to the floor, and that's when I heard a muffled gunshot. From the sound of it, I figured it had hit something soft – flesh, internal organs. A human being. Somehow, I knew Davi had taken the worst of it. I heard a 'Fuck' and the sound of panting, broken up by moans. I looked: César was dragging himself out from under Davi and a crimson stain was growing on the back of the prince's grey shirt. Davi applied pressure to the wound on his abdomen and moaned. While I tried to take back control of my legs, César had forgotten about me and was apologising to his boss, friend, half-brother, or whatever they were to each other, for having let a woman get between them and things ending up that way. I imagined him holding Davi in his arms like a pietà, since I couldn't see anything. I heard sniffing. I heard a feeble 'Don't let me die', then an even feebler 'To a hospital' and I guessed that Davi was losing consciousness. I couldn't stay there any longer. I shot towards the exit; César sprinted after me. I flew through the door, running barefoot, without even watching where I was treading, my feet filthy, crusty, frozen, and none of it mattered. I knew he was coming to hunt me down. Suddenly I heard the heavy thud of someone falling and looked back.

When I saw Lucinda and Grazi holding down César, my brain finally gave itself permission to switch off. I don't remember whether I spoke to them or not. I don't remember a word they said.

I remember that we went into the living room shortly after calling 190. Graziane approached Davi, felt his pulse; he was unconscious and had tears in his eyes; there was still a pulse, though it was weak. From the amount of blood on the floor and the place the bullet had gone in, we soon realised how it was going to end. We left and went to wait on the porch, despite the cold. I was no longer barefoot: Grazi had given me her boots.

One of the cops removed the gag they'd put on César. While he was being taken to the car he remained quiet, perhaps so as not to incriminate himself. The gun was gathered and taken to the forensics lab. A coroner took flash photos. Lucinda had the presence of mind to photograph the scene of the crime as well, to defend ourselves in case there was any attempt to incriminate us.

Graziane, Lucinda and I walked to the gate, where they had left the hired car, in which we would follow the police to the station.

As I sit in the passenger seat it dawns on me that, if Lucinda had access to my spreadsheet, then she must know I'm on the game by now. I look at her, all nervous. She understands my look and puts me at ease:

'I didn't tell Mum about that part. She's on her way back to Brazil, by the way.'

'Great,' I reply.

In the car, on the way to the station, we conclude that it still isn't the right time to tell our mother what I really do for a living. I'd say that my casual sex with Davi had made him obsessed with me, wanting a relationship, and when I refused he had sent his servant to kidnap me in order to try to convince me. Lying to your lawyer is a classic move; lying to your mother even more so.

I worry about César's gun, which Lucinda touched. César could twist the whole story, one of us could be accused of having fired it, especially if he had the backing of the Rodrigues family's lawyers. But Davi's father would never again consider César 'part of the family' if it became clear that he had killed his only son. The theory I had come up with came back to me, that César might be Davi's half-brother. In that case, things could get even more dangerous.

Listening to my concerns, Lucinda offers me a pill from her bag to help me relax. I say I don't want to relax, I want to have fire in my veins for when I press charges, because you can bet it won't be a walk in the park. I accept a painkiller instead.

Inside the station, however, the curly-haired officer listens and accepts our complaint, charging César with the crimes of kidnap, assault, false imprisonment, attempted femicide and some others. She only refuses to press for rape – 'What's the point, if the accused can no longer defend himself?' Lucinda and I persist and I repeat how it happened. The officer proposes to record that I was raped after being induced to ingest drugs – not 'induced', I correct her, 'coerced'– and that therefore I cannot say for sure who committed the act. We argue next to the scribe. In the background I see a secretary walk past with a grin on his face. I refuse to sign the complaint as it is. Then the officer urges me to have my forensic examination regarding the other accusations. Davi's family has already been informed; his father is coming here in his private jet, and I don't want to run into him.

It's already past midnight and I'm taken to forensics in a nearby town, where they take photos of my beaten and bruised body and ask a lot of questions. There are visible marks from Davi's fingers around my neck, under my hair. I hadn't realised how hard he'd squeezed my neck; maybe he'd done it again when I was doped up. My face burns from all the slaps I received from Davi, which left no marks. But the bump on my head, the contusions, the bruises and the scratches: it's all noted. They check a possible cracked rib, which, in fact, had begun to hurt after César punched me in the stomach, and they also take note of something on my shoulder and arm. Then the forensics officer takes me to the hospital. I undergo some tests there, but as the results only come out the following morning I ask for a sedative: they give me one and I'm out like a light. Lucinda and Grazi take over. When I wake up in the morning, my mother is by my side. She hugs me tight, taking care because of my condition, a piece of paper in her hand brushing my hair from behind.

'I made that weaselly officer change the charges,' she says, shaking the paper before my face. 'You now have the right to the rape kit. And, if you want, to another forensic examination.'

I don't. I take the pills she gives me, get on whatever machines they ask me to and then re-enter my induced sleep. The local press, consisting of a journalist and a photographer, appear, hoping to get into the ward to interview me. Lucinda and my mother shoo them away with legal threats, but they continue to pace around the reception. Grazi doesn't leave my side. When I wake up, we decide to tell my mother about our relationship, knowing that these horrible circumstances could be strangely favourable to our acceptance as a couple. My mother seems a bit on edge, but then she says, 'My dear, I love you, that's all that matters. How long have you been together? Everything's OK, everything's OK,' she repeats, hugging me and Grazi, while Lucinda looks at us askance from by the door, the ominous bearer of the other truth, that of my secret profession. For now, I'm not considering revealing it, but I know that someday it will be unavoidable.

Finally, I'm let out. Mum says she's going to stay in the town a while longer, to follow the next steps: 'I know the score in small towns: if someone doesn't keep on top of a case like this, anything could happen.' With her phone she takes new photos of my bruises, which are now even more pronounced, and says she's going to the local forensics department. Lucinda will take Grazi and me to São Paulo in her hired car.

I get up slowly, take a shower and get into the new clothes Lucinda has bought me from a local shop. I, who have so scorned family, am witnessing my own family, the blood one and the one I've chosen, rescue me and look after me. I feel divided between the loyalty I owe to myself as an independent being, self-sufficient and desiring distance from humanity, and the loyalty I owe to those who, at the end of the day, made my actual survival possible. I feel myself changing, though into what I don't yet know.

As we walk past the hospital reception counter, I wave to Rosali, one of the nurses who looked after me. She waves back. Her eyes are huge, as if she has seen a ghost in me. I am struck with the sensation that I meant something to her, that perhaps she has also gone through what I did. What stories would the women of those muffled cities say if someone asked them – and wanted to hear?

Graziane goes out with my mother to distract the small troupe of reporters still waiting to pounce, having been informed of my release. Lucinda and I leave the hospital through a different door and go to the car, which is parked beneath a tree on the other side of the square. Grazi is waiting for us one street down, in front of a café.

'You know,' says Lucinda, 'if she's going to be your lawyer, you'll need to come clean about what you really do.'

214

'Not right now.'

'Of course not right now. Eventually. Whenever you're ready. And I'll help you, stand by your side. She'll understand.'

I tear up a bit, more because of her heartfelt tone than her words. I glance her way: 'Thanks, Lucy. That means a lot.'

'No worries.' She pauses, then turns back to me. 'Do you have everything you need? Painkillers and all? There's a pharmacy right over there.' She points.

I nod, smiling at her clumsy efforts to be a better sister. I wipe my eyes with the back of my hand as we go around the kids playing football in front of a Catholic church. An evangelical storefront church sits on the opposite corner, where our car is parked.

Suddenly, another head pops up next to Lucinda's, a man whose skin tone suggests Lebanese ancestry and a beard that, in sharp contrast, is almost white. He seems familiar. At first, I think he's a doctor from the hospital, but when I look at his face I don't recognise him.

'I beg your pardon. My name is Omar Rodrigues,' he says, looking at me. 'I'm Davi's father. He just passed away.'

'Could easily have been me,' I reply, walking quicker.

'He was too good for this world.'

He kidnapped me, assaulted me and raped me, I think about saying, but don't. But it's as if I had because he *replies*, almost shouting, from behind me:

'He was sick! Get it? He was sick.'

I say nothing. Does that make everything OK? Everything I went through? I want to get into the car right now,

215

but Lucinda is taking a while to find the key in her huge bag.

'Viviana,' Omar says, and I look into his red, tear-stained face. 'Davi was my only son. My only heir. Now everything I have… will die with me.'

I remain silent, looking at the passenger door, while Lucinda, on the other side, finally unlocks the car. When I pull the handle to open the door, he grabs my arm.

'I came to ask you… please. If my grandson is in there, don't get rid of him.'

I yank my arm free, sit down and slam the door shut. He lowers his head to window height and shouts:

'You hear me? My son is not a rapist. You will not get rid of my grandson! I will have justice!'

Lucinda accelerates. As we drive away, Davi's father remains static, standing in the middle of the square, shouting the same thing over and over. Especially *justice*.

ACKNOWLEDGEMENTS

To Anna Luiza, Luciana, Miguel and everyone at the Villas-Boas & Moss agency for their work in making this book happen.

To everyone at Companhia das Letras, especially Luara França, Alice Sant'Anna and Luiz Schwarcz, for believing in this book when it was merely an idea.

To my dearest Rodrigo Deodoro, Amanda Miranda, Helloara Ravani, Sandra Campos, Raphael Montes, Stephanie Fernandes, Daniel Lima, Osmar Shineidr, Fernanda Celleghin, Janaína Tokitaka, Janaína Ananias, Camila Dias da Cruz, Mônica Surrage, Laís Alcântara, Luciana Tamaki, Márcio Pinheiro, Cíntia Marcucci, Thiago Straus Rabelo, João Cezar de Castro Rocha, Amanda Giordano and Maria Clara Drummond for your beta readings, suggestions and moral/logistical support during the creation of this book.

To everyone who, through their careful work, helped make the English version of *Nothing Can Hurt You Now* shine: Rahul Bery, Harriet Wade, Kirsten Chapman, Elodie Olson-Coons, Ameenah Khan, among many others.

AVAILABLE AND COMING SOON
FROM PUSHKIN VERTIGO

Jonathan Ames

You Were Never Really Here
A Man Named Doll
The Wheel of Doll

Simone Campos

Nothing Can Hurt You Now

Zijin Chen

Bad Kids

Maxine Mei-Fung Chung

The Eighth Girl

Candas Jane Dorsey

The Adventures of Isabel
What's the Matter with Mary Jane?

Margot Douaihy

Scorched Grace

Joey Hartstone

The Local

Seraina Kobler

Deep Dark Blue

Elizabeth Little

Pretty as a Picture

Jack Lutz

London in Black

Steven Maxwell

All Was Lost

Callum McSorley

Squeaky Clean

Louise Mey

The Second Woman

John Kåre Raake

The Ice

RV Raman

A Will to Kill
Grave Intentions
Praying Mantis

Paula Rodríguez

Urgent Matters

Nilanjana Roy

Black River

John Vercher

Three-Fifths
After the Lights Go Out

Emma Viskic

Resurrection Bay
And Fire Came Down
Darkness for Light
Those Who Perish

Yulia Yakovleva

Punishment of a Hunter
Death of the Red Rider